The Bedroom Bandit

A novel

By

Richard Jeanty

RJ Publications, LLC

Newark, New Jersey

The characters and events in this book are fictitious. Any resemblance to actual persons, living or dead, is purely coincidental.

RJ Publications
rjeantay@yahoo.com
www.rjpublications.com
Copyright © 2009 by Richard Jeanty
All Rights Reserved
ISBN 978-0978637361

Printed in Canada

March 2009

1-2-3-4-5-6-7-8-9-10-11

"The Bedroom Bandit"

BY

Richard Jeanty

Acknowledgement

I would like to thank all the usual suspects who have supported me through my writing career and other endeavors. By now I shouldn't have to mention your names anymore.

To my baby girl, Rishanna, I can never leave your name out. I love you unconditionally. Thanks for being such a wonderful little girl. You continue to brighten my days and put a smile on my face every time I need one. I love you.

Special "thanks" goes out to pops, Serge Jeanty, for not leaving me behind in this world. You're still my man.

I would especially like to thank Michaelle Myrthil, Yolander Boston, LaQuita Adams and my special new editor, who did a great job with this book, Nicole Scales. Thanks for the special help.

Thanks go out to all the book clubs and readers who continue to inspire me to get better with each book. Thanks to the staff at The Literary Joint. But a special shout out goes to my man, MO and Phil for their great hustle. I can't forget about Nick and Keisha for all their dedication. I would like to give a big shout- out to the street vendors, especially Pogo, Henry and Abou, and all the booksellers around the country and all over the world for keeping the world in tune with our literature. Thanks to all the book retailers and distributors who make it possible for our books to reach the people.

A special shout-out goes to Barbara Harris and all the New York book vendors and entrepreneurs. A big shout-out goes out to my nephews and nieces as well as my brothers and sisters. And last but not least, I would like to thank my fellow writers for making reading fun again for our people. I hope that I didn't leave anyone out. My mind gets crowded, sometimes. I must be part of the "Hey Mon Family," I have so many jobs.

Introduction

Usually, I'm able to write a decent introduction to my books, but I seem to be having a harder time this time around. However, I'll try to give it a go.

Often times, life leads us in so many directions and sometimes we have no idea whether it's right or left. The decision to the right path, most of the time, is determined by money. But money doesn't always equate to right or just. We live in a society where we are forced to be driven by our wealth and not necessarily our talent. Many talented authors, artists, singers, painters, comics and, actors have never received the kind of accolades they deserve. However, that doesn't mean they're not worthy. Money supposedly represents power and success, but there are quite a few people out there with money without power and if jumping out of a building is the only answer after losing some, or all of a person's money, I don't need that kind of success.

Sometimes, we are forced to ignore our talent due to the lack of respect or the need for basic survival in a society driven by money. However, it doesn't mean that we won't end up on the right path, eventually. Destiny can't be avoided. A talented person might have to detour a few times before getting to the right path, but he'll get there, somehow. It's already written.

I hope that we can all find our paths in life and we can use our given talent to be a productive part of society. Most of all, I hope that we don't stop dreaming and hoping because President Obama certainly did not and look at where it has gotten him.

I don't set out to teach any lessons in my books, but somehow they always end up with one. I guess that's a part of who I am and my destiny. I also never thought that I could write ten books in such a short amount of time, but I did it. I really couldn't tell you how. I hope that you can still enjoy my work and I appreciate the support.

Reach for the highest goal possible and achieve!

The Best Job in the World?

I'm sitting in this hospital with a broken neck, two broken arms and a broken foot wondering if I deserved what happened to me. In some way, I think I did, but I'm not completely to blame. It takes two to tangle, but my tangling ways got my ass whipped in the worst way.

A few months ago, I never saw this coming. I was deep inside Tara digging into every inch of her pussy while her husband was hard at work trying to earn a living to pay for the posh lifestyle in the suburbs that she enjoyed so much. Tara was just one of my many clients. She was the usual arm candy type of housewife that you would find in most suburbs. She was Italian and her honey complexion and sister-like shape revealed that I wasn't the only brother to ever visit her terrain. She had a nice shape, petite body type and she was as gorgeous as she wanted to be with long dark hair.

She didn't even know me from atom. All she knew was that I was there to do a job and that I was good at what I did. She teased me with her bare shoulders as she ran her fingers up and down her chest. Underneath her silk robe, was her birthday suit. A little flashing soon revealed her shaven pussy and excited clit, waiting to get licked by me. Whatever she wanted she was going to get. Tara threw her arms around my shoulders to feel the muscular tone of my physique. She didn't talk much. She was all about action. She led me straight to the kitchen and told me, "I want you to fuck me on the counter." She had a beautiful kitchen and counter top that I could work with. I lifted her up and sat her on the counter while her feet dangled. When I spread apart her thighs, I could hear her pussy calling my name, as she instantly became moist. I felt like Lexington Steele as I bent down and started licking her inner thighs all the way up to her pussy. All I heard were her moans and groans as my tongue made contact with her pussy lips. They were a little longer than usual, like too many men had sucked on them. I proceeded to suck them lightly while sticking a finger inside her. Her pussy was dripping wet as my finger invaded her private territory. She leaned back on the counter and I attacked her perky breasts with my hands. My fingers ran circles around her erected nipples. "Fuck me already!" she screamed out.

I was more than ready to fuck her. As customary, I pulled out my extra large Magnum condom and rolled it down my thick long dick. I pulled Tara forward, toward the edge of the counter and I started fucking her. Suddenly, she wasn't so silent anymore. "Fuck me! Fuck the shit outta me!" she yelled. I was about a good eight inches in as she screamed for more. The more she screamed the more fierce my strokes became and I wanted to tear Tara's pussy up. With one finger rubbing her clit, I was fucking the hell out of Tara. Strokes after strokes after strokes, she kept begging for more. I pulled her ass forward off the counter and held on to her legs while her back rested on the counter top. My entire dick was banging her walls and Tara was on her way to heaven. "That's it. Keep fucking me," she commanded. Sweat was pouring down my body as I stroked Tara as hard as I could before she pulled her body toward me and held me while she trembled in ecstasy.

That was my usual gig and I got paid very well for doing it. I was "The Bedroom Bandit" and I was damn good at my job. My hospitalization was also the danger that came along with my job. First, you need to learn the whole story, so you can have a better understanding of my predicament.

Stay Down Boy

You're probably saying to yourself that with a name like 'The Bedroom Bandit' I probably deserved everything I got, right? Well, first, it will take me some time to explain how I got my name. I was a victim of circumstance at the age of sixteen. Like most teenagers, I was horny twenty four-seven and I walked around with a hard dick like I was born with a third leg. I don't know what it was that made me so horny all the time, but I was. I can still remember the first day that Ms. Charles noticed my package. She was the neighbor who lived on the first floor apartment below us. My mother and I lived in a three-family house in Mattapan, Massachusetts, which is an urban part of Boston. We lived on the third floor and one of my best friends, Kevin, lived on the second floor with his family. I was going downstairs to pick up the mail and all of a sudden, the snake in my pants started to unfold for no reason. To this day, I still can't remember what I was thinking about that made my dick so hard. Just as I reached the last step, Ms. Charles opened her door and the bulge in my pants couldn't be denied.

That shit was so obvious I was embarrassed. I was hoping that Ms. Charles did not think I was a perverted teenager who got hard every time I saw her. A smile flashed across her face when her eyes met my bulge and out of the blue, she said to me, "David, I didn't know you were so blessed." Being the ignorant teenager that I was, I didn't make much of her comment. "I pray to God every night, I guess you can say I'm blessed," I answered. "Yes, you are and I'm gonna keep an eye on you from now on," she retorted. I ran outside to the front door and picked up the mail that was spread all over the floor. The house didn't have any mailboxes. There was a mail slot at the bottom of the door and everyone was responsible for picking up his or her own mail once the mailman put it through the slot. I sorted out my Mom's mail and I headed back upstairs as Ms. Charles left with this devilish look in her eyes as she grinned at me.

When I got back upstairs, I felt like I was caught with my pants down. I tried to make my dick go down, but I had no dick control. My dick would just spring up on its own and there was nothing I could do about it. The fact that I carried around nine and a half inches of blood flow in my pants at the age of sixteen was kind hard on me as well at times. Even at school, it was difficult sometimes because I would get hard and have to put my book bag in front of me to hide it from the rest of the world.

Of course, I was still a virgin at the age of sixteen, but I masturbated religiously. I was able to get my hand on this old Hustler magazine that I kept under my mattress. It was a tension reliever. Ever since I reached puberty, my mother had made it clear to me that she didn't want to become a grandmother in her thirties and I had better not even think about having sex with a girl before I was eighteen. And my mother was serious, too. Even when I was in my room jerking off, I felt she was watching me and telling me to get my hand off my dick. My mom didn't hide anything from me. She started talking to me about sex and teenage pregnancy very early in my life. She almost had me believe that if I humped a girl the wrong way with my clothes on, there was a possibility that she might get pregnant and my life would be ruined. She gave me a lot of misinformation, which led to my defiant sexual journey and into the arms of Ms. Charles.

The Unit

My mother and father divorced when I was ten years old. It was an amicable divorce, but my father didn't come around enough to spend time with me. It was almost like he divorced me as well. But my mother picked up the slack the best way she knew how. My father remarried and had a couple of children with his new wife and acted like I was a part-time child. It made no difference to me because my mother loved me more than enough to make up for the love that I didn't get from my father.

My mother wasn't the type to stress my dad out about child support or alimony, even though he was ordered to pay her one hundred and fifty dollars a week after the divorce settlement. I'm not really sure how much of that money my mother really saw because she worked a lot of overtime at her job to help pay the bills and maintain the family. I never once heard her complain. She was a strong woman who managed to do it on her own without showing any bitterness towards my father. However, I did receive special gifts on my birthday and Christmas time every year from my father. He also occasionally brought me a couple of pairs of Jeans and sneakers when he felt like it. What I wanted more was to spend time with him when I was a kid.

It seemed like my father forgot that I was his first child after he remarried. Sure, he had another son and a daughter with his new wife, but I was his first and he didn't treat me like that. I never even had the chance to spend a lot of time with my siblings. My father was always short on time and he thought it was special that he remembered my birthday every year and bought me a gift every Christmas. By the time I reached sixteen years old, I was no longer interested in his gifts and I saw him for what he was, a conniving liar. No wonder my mother caught him cheating on her with his current wife.

When I was ten years old, my mother worked the morning shift at her job. Since she was a nurse, there wasn't much flexibility with her schedule. She would wake up at six in the morning to get me ready for school and she'd be waiting at three thirty in the afternoon at the bus stop to pick me up everyday. She would drop me off at my grandmother's house on the weekends so she could pick up some extra hours of overtime at work. Aside from sleeping, my mother spent the rest of her time with me. She would take me out on little picnics at Houghton's Pond in Milton, to Franklin Park in Dorchester to ride my bike and when she had extra money, she would take me to Water Country in New Hampshire or Six Flags. My mother provided me with a fun and nurturing childhood.

My mother was also a strict disciplinarian who had the potential to unleash a serious ass whipping on me. I managed to never find out how serious she could whip my ass by staying in line all the time. As much as my mother tried to compensate for my father not being there most of the time, I still felt that as a young boy, I needed a father figure in my life. It is essential that young boys, especially black boys, have a positive male role model in their lives. Well, I couldn't cry over spilled milk, so I found the next best thing in what I thought was a great male role model, my uncle.

The closest thing that I found in a father figure was my uncle Joe, who was my mother's brother. What a father figure he was. Uncle Joe was a few years younger than my mother and about sixteen years older than me. I idolized the man. I wanted to be everything that Uncle Joe was, smooth, handsome, a Casanova and a ladies' man. Uncle Joe wore the finest clothes, drove the nicest cars and was adored by the entire family. On the surface, he was the perfect man. He went straight to college after high school and graduated summa cum laude. Then he went on to get an MBA from Harvard University. He made the family proud, but Uncle Joe had a fear, which was commitment. I later found out that he wanted to wait til he was too old to get married. Of course, I'm being sarcastic.

Being suave, debonair and handsome had its perks and Uncle Joe made that perfectly clear to me. "You're a Sinclair and Sinclair men always get their way with the ladies," he used to say. My mother's maiden name is Sinclair but my last name is Richardson, named after my dad. I'm also a junior, which sometimes pisses me off. If my dad cared so much to name me after him, why the hell didn't he want to spend time with me? I would ask myself. I decided to absorb everything that Uncle Joe dished out to get back at my father. He and my uncle were like night and day. They couldn't stand each other. My mother once told me a story about Uncle Joe beating up my daddy because he had put his hand on my mother. Uncle Joe wasn't just a scholar; he was a well-balanced man who could navigate his way through the hood as well as corporate America.

Obtaining a job making close to six figures right out of college, Uncle Joe was the epitome of success and every black woman in the hood wanted a piece of him. He called himself prime real estate and he was grooming me to be just like him. Even though I wished I could've spent more time with my father, Uncle Joe more than made up for his lack of presence. I was driven around in a convertible Saab, which was one of the most popular cars in the late eighties and Uncle Joe brought me to the mall more often than Santa Claus delivered gifts to kids during Christmas. I also found out the relationship that my uncle and I shared was beneficial to both of us. Women saw him as the caring uncle who took care of and spent time with his neglected nephew, and I got spoiled like a little rich brat by him. My uncle was always generous with me. Sometimes my mother would get mad when he brought me back home with bags full of clothing, but that's who he was. At least, that was how he presented himself to the family.

The fact that I was a very handsome little boy worked a lot to my uncle's benefit and mine, too. Women were always swarming over me at the mall, pulling on my cheeks and telling my uncle how cute I was. "He came from great genes," he would tell them and by the time we left the mall, he would have ten to fifteen phone numbers. Sure, he used me, but he reciprocated with the gifts that he bought me. As a child, I felt that my uncle was the richest man in the world, a little too rich sometimes. He was treated like a celebrity by everyone in the family and even more so by women. I guess a degree from Harvard seems to be so unattainable, so when one of us finally gets one, it's almost like reaching godly status. The minute Harvard University rolled off my uncle's tongue, the phone numbers started flying. Women sometimes used their eyeliner to write down their numbers and some acted like they were begging for a call. It was a variety of women too, but mostly professionals. I never thought that women could be so desperate.

Player in Training

One of the first things my uncle emphasized when I spent time with him was the importance of a great education. "Women are impressed by educated, intelligent and revered men, and that's why it's important for you to always get good grades in school and make sure you're at the top of your class," he would tell me. Hearing those words from my uncle all the time, I had no choice but to be a great student at Latin Academy High School. My uncle had no problem rewarding me for my hard work and I felt that he was genuinely proud of me. He treated me like his apprentice and the son that he never had. My uncle also warned me to stay away from the young girls at my school because they would interfere with my goals and dreams. "You have to dream bigger than those young chicks at your school. If you start wasting your time with them, you'll also start to let your grades slide and you will lose focus. Women will always want your time, but right now you should try to spend time with women who have limited time." My uncle was like a scientist to me. He was always dropping science and I took in his every word. "Women chase men with money, not the other way around," he emphasized.

"You see, Ms. Charles, who lives on the first floor of your house, I was gonna do her because she's been jocking me for a while, but I wanted to leave her for you. She's going to be the woman who's gonna teach you everything you need to know in the bedroom," he told me one day. "Why do you say that?" I asked. "Well, she's probably in her thirties and I have never seen a man at her house. I know for a fact that she gets horny and the closest dick supply she has is you. The fact that your mother owns the house where she lives is also an attraction. It's almost like saying that she's gonna get a return for paying her rent on time every month." The only thing I could say was, "Wow!" My uncle seemed to be right on the money because Ms. Charles was a single mother of two young kids. She worked a lot of hours to take care of those kids and I never saw any man leaving her house and she was smiling at me a lot.

My uncle spoon-fed me a lot about Ms. Charles and I knew it was just a matter of time before I was invited in for my first sexual romp. Planning was essential to get to Ms. Charles' panties. My uncle helped me plan the everything. "Junior," he would call me, "This is what you're gonna do. You're gonna sit on the front porch and wait until you see Ms. Charles walking down the street on her way to the house, and just as she's coming through the door, you're gonna go downstairs in your boxers to pick up the mail. She's gonna be so stressed from work, you're gonna look like Michael Jordan to her. And since I know that she hasn't been getting any because she keeps blowing up my phone, I know she's gonna give in to you to release some of that stress." I was seventeen years old and horny as a toad when my uncle was telling me all this. I took my uncle's advice and I stayed away from the girls at my school. Ms. Charles was about to get it because I was a sexually frustrated teenager. "Junior, you can't compare a woman to a little girl. A woman will teach you how to please her, and she will train you to be the best lover that you can be and the pussy's gonna be the bomb most of the time. I think Kelly has some good pussy and you're gonna be in for a treat," Uncle Joe told me. I was not used to hearing her first name, Kelly. I always called her Ms. Charles. After I reached puberty, my uncle and I became very comfortable with each other and he talked to me like I was one of his boys and I liked that. To me, it was his way of showing respect by treating me like a young man. I grew a few inches taller, my voice got a little deeper and my uncle acknowledged it by treating me as his equal during conversations.

The day finally came. I could see Ms. Charles strutting down the street in her corporate suit looking as good as a Godiva candy bar. It was a good thing that my mother switched her work schedule to the evening shift from three to eleven. That gave me plenty of time to get my groove on with Ms. Charles. Ms. Charles worked a nine-to-five, she got home everyday at six o'clock and she picked up her children from her parents house at eight everyday. The window of opportunity was two hours and I wanted to make sure that I capitalized on that. My dick was rock hard from watching Ms. Charles and I knew only two things could happen, I could embarrass myself by going downstairs in my boxers with a rock hard dick or I can be invited into Ms. Charles' apartment and have the best sex of my life. It was a risk I was willing to take based on my uncle's assessment of the situation.

I could hear Ms. Charles forcing her key to open the first lock on the main entrance door and I needed to catch her before she got to her apartment door. I came running downstairs busting my ass, tripping on the last staircase and landing on my back. I could see the concerned look on her face through the second glass door that separates us from the cruel outside world. An additional door for some reason makes black people feel safer in the hood, just as the extra locks are supposed to be additional protection in the projects. I fell on my ass so hard, my hard dick slipped into a coma and the blood flow went somewhere else. I could feel the pain running through my body. "Are you alright?" Ms. Charles asked. Hell no! I wasn't all right, but I needed to play tough because she definitely wouldn't want to be with a sissy. I wanted to jump to my feet on my own, but I couldn't. Ms. Charles could sense my attempt at being macho, so she extended her hand to me and told me that it was okay to ask for help. She brought me into her house and got an ice pack to put on my back.

It was my first time ever inside Ms. Charles' house. I was laying on my stomach on the couch in the living room and I could see the rest of the house from front to back except for her room and the kids' rooms. It was a three-bedroom apartment and Ms. Charles kept it very neat. She had a tan leather sectional living room set with an ottoman, coffee table, and end tables to match. In the kitchen, I could see a breakfast table with four chairs, and in her dining room, she had a huge mahogany china cabinet with matching table and six chairs and two armchairs at each end of the table. Even the pastel color paint on the wall of Ms. Charles' apartment was impressive.

There is a God

As I lay on Ms. Charles' couch, I no longer felt the pain on my back, because she left her bedroom door cracked as she changed from her work clothes to a robe and slippers. I could see the matching black undergarment that held her perky breasts together and the bikini underwear that comforted her nice round booty through her skirt. It was a time when bikini underwear was as hot as a thong before the thong was invented. "Are you still in pain?" she yelled out to me from her bedroom. "It's getting better." My dick was starting to get hard again and it was a good thing that I was laying on my stomach. At that point, it would've been disrespectful to let Ms. Charles see my erection because she had taken on a motherly role to help nurture my wound. After securing the robe around her body, Ms. Charles stepped out of her room and asked me if I wanted anything to drink. I was already drunk by her beauty, so I declined. For a woman who had two children, Ms. Charles had a body tighter than most of the girls at my high school. Her robe only came down to her knees and for the first time I got lost in her legs. I imagined licking her legs all the way up to her thigh as she walked to the kitchen to get something to drink. I didn't have any experience licking anything, but I had seen enough pictures in that old Hustler magazine that made me feel that licking a woman was essential to pleasing her.

Those pictures showed the men with their tongue extended to the top of this little thing above the vagina, which I later found out is called a clitoris and I wanted to lick hers. I wish she would drop that robe and come to the couch to let me get a whiff of that sweet smelling pussy of hers, I thought to myself. I was salivating like it was my favorite meal and I didn't care anymore about how she'd feel if she saw my hard nine inch dick. I rolled over onto my back to watch her. Ms. Charles caught me peeping at her, but more importantly, she caught the huge bulge in my underwear and said, "Boy! Are we excited today?" I didn't know how to respond, so I stayed quiet. "Dave, is there something that you would like to do?" she asked. Yeah, I wanted to tell her that I would love to jump her bones, but my sexual vocabulary hadn't yet developed.

"How about I go take a shower and we can discuss it when I get out," she said. I was wishing that she would invite me into the shower with her. She came out the bathroom butt naked thirty seconds after stepping in and said, "As a matter of fact, how about you join me in the shower?" I was gonna pinch myself to see if I was dreaming but pinching wouldn't be enough, so I bit my arms and I could feel my teeth penetrating my skin confirming that I was wide awake and God was about to answer a prayer that I had been saying since I was sixteen years old. I ran to the bathroom and dropped my boxers to the floor. My nine inches stood up in front of me like I was that kid who carried the flag in front of the school's marching band.

Ms. Charles didn't shave her crotch like most of the women I had seen in Hustler. Her curly pubic hair looked sexy and I wanted to touch it. As we stepped in the shower, she copped a feel of my ass and said, "Nice and tight, I like that." I figured one good turn deserved another. I reached my hand out and palmed the most perfect ass that I had ever seen. As a matter of fact, it was the only ass that I had ever seen live. I was also lost in her succulent breasts. I felt like a puppy waiting to be fed. The water was nice and I was hoping that I'd get a chance to turn up the heat a little in the shower with Ms. Charles. She started to lather my chest with soap with her hands and I swore I was gonna bust a nut from her touching my chest. And then the unexpected happened, Ms. Charles grabbed hold of my nine inches and before she had a chance to even thoroughly rub the soap on the head, I exploded in her hand. That shit was so embarrassing. I had no dick control whatsoever. Ms. Charles, however, consoled me like I had just lost my pet dog. "It's okay, David, you don't have to be embarrassed. This has happen with grown ass men that I have been with. I understand." Ms. Charles even jerked me off a little so I could get a complete nut.

The soothing touch of Ms. Charles' hand was comforting to my penis. I felt an instant surge of energy and I was standing nine inches tall again without missing a beat. As the water hit my chest and rolled down my body, I could feel a different kind of warmth. It was sensual and it came from a soft place. I started to shiver when I noticed Ms. Charles' tongue navigating my abdomen on her way down to my crotch. She even looked sexy with a plastic shower cap on her head. I didn't know the etiquette for receiving a blowjob, so I looked a little odd with my hands on my waist. I stood there like I had just conquered Mount Rushmore. Ms. Charles continued to amaze me with the movement of her tongue in unison with her hands. She had the tip of my penis in her mouth licking it slowly while she massaged my balls with her hands. I feared another quick nut was coming again, but somehow I managed to tighten up my body and was able to enjoy Ms. Charles' treat.

I swear I wish I had a camera so I could videotape the everything because I knew that none of my friends or even my uncle was going to believe that Ms. Charles gave me a blowjob. Back then, blowjobs were taboo, only freaks did it openly, and I instantly labeled Ms. Charles as a freak for sucking my dick. Even the cool water hitting my skin couldn't keep the sweat beads from forming on my brow. I was hot as hell, but I didn't know what to do. I felt like a kid waiting for Ms. Charles to yell out the directions to me, but she said nothing. Her actions spoke louder than her words. She must've sucked me off for a good ten minutes before she made her way back up and started kissing me ever so gently. Her tongue was soft and sweet, but I felt like I was sucking my own dick by kissing her. My adolescent mind didn't know anything different. She had just given me a blowjob and now she was kissing me; that was a no-no in my book. I would definitely keep that part of our sexual romp to myself when I speak to my friends about it. I was immature and whatever I heard from my peers, I took to heart. However, I had an experienced uncle who always set me straight whenever I was wrong.

While Ms. Charles kissed me, I wanted to insert myself inside her. I spread open her legs and I took my dick and placed it between her legs while truly believing that I had just penetrated her. She held her legs tight as I humped back and forth. I thought I was in heaven. Five minutes later, I was coming and asking Ms. Charles if it was good for her. "What do you mean if it was good to me?" she asked. "The sex we just had," I answered. "We haven't had sex yet," she said. "I was just inside you. You mean to tell me you didn't feel anything?" I asked her. I could feel another embarrassing moment coming on, so I braced myself. "Look Dave, you have a lot to learn and I don't mind teaching you, but we're not gonna do that in the shower. Let's dry up and take this to the bedroom." I don't know if I was supposed to feel embarrassed with her statement or if I was supposed to be excited. Anyway, I dried off very fast and went to her bed to lie down butt naked with my dick reaching for the ceiling.

When Ms. Charles entered he room, she explained to me that I was never inside her. As a matter of fact, she was moaning because her clit was rubbing against my dick while I humped her. At seventeen years old, I had the best sex teacher in the entire world. Ms. Charles turned the lights on in her room and spread her legs open and started showing me the different parts of her pussy. As patient a student as I wanted to be, I couldn't help myself. I told Ms. Charles that I wanted to hurry up and have sex with her before she had to go pick up her children. "Dave, a lady does not like a man who wants to rush things. You have to take your time to please a woman and you have to allow that woman to teach you a thing or two about her body. Not everything that you do is gonna work for every woman that you're with," she told me. Ms. Charles was schooling me and I decided to be the obedient student and learn.

First lesson: the pleasure zone; Ms. Charles directed me to her clitoris and taught me how to properly eat a woman until she succumbed to my tongue prowess. I ate Ms. Charles' pussy until my mouth started to hurt. I felt joy hearing Ms. Charles calling my name while I was eating her. Every time I got a little rough with my tongue, Ms. Charles would tell me to ease up and taught me how to do it right. Her moaning got me excited and I wanted to become the best pussy eater there was in the world. At one point, I felt like Ms. Charles didn't want me to penetrate her, but I was wrong. After eating her until I almost took my last breath, Ms. Charles directed me to insert a finger inside her. She was already wet, so I had no problem sticking my middle finger inside her. It felt snug and I kept sticking it in and out. The moaning continued and I added an extra finger for more pleasure. By then, I developed a nice little rhythm and I could see Ms. Charles was enjoying my tactics. The moans were louder and she also started to groan as well. I felt this rush coming over me. I pulled my finger out and tried to stick my dick inside Ms. Charles. She quickly put a damper on my plans as she stopped me in my track and asked me to wrap it up. "Wrap it up with what?" I asked. I had no idea that, "wrap it up," meant wearing a condom.

After pulling out a condom from her top drawer and rolling it down my erected little man, she took my dick this time and inserted it inside her. I could feel the warmth of her juices flowing around my dick and it felt like heaven was near. I was finally in the pussy and I wanted to hump as hard as I could. However, every time I tried to hump her hard I kept slipping and sliding out of her. Slowing down the motion of my strokes, Ms. Charles started yelling, "Right there! That's the spot. Keep doing what you're doing. The sensitive sensation of rubber to skin kept me from another premature ejaculation episode. I stroked Ms. Charles until she started screaming, "I'm cumming. Yes! Oh shit! You're making me cum!" I just continued with what I was doing as Ms. Charles' body went into convulsion. By the time I was ready to bust another nut, sweat was pouring down both of us and we had to go back in the shower to rinse off.

My Friends

It was official. I busted my very first nut with a woman who was mature and experienced. Now it was up to me to keep my affair with Ms. Charles from my mother. She would kick Ms. Charles out without a second thought if she had any inclination that I was screwing her. Before running my mouth to any of my friends, I needed to consult with my uncle first. Rumors have a way of spreading throughout the hood and the last thing I wanted was to cause any embarrassment to Ms. Charles. Not only that, there was so much more that I needed to learn from her sexually, I just couldn't risk it. She had to have perceived me as a mature young man for her to sleep with me, so I needed to keep my mouth shut out of respect for her. The temptation to brag to the first person that I knew was circling around in my head. My boy, Kevin, lived a little too close on the second floor below me and my other boy, Rammell, lived up the street on Selden street while I lived on West Selden. The three of us had been best friends since the day we started the Murphy Elementary School together. From there, we went to Thompson Middle School together, then Rammell and I went on to attend Latin Academy after taking the entrance exam and passing with flying colors. Kevin didn't care much about taking a 4-hour exam to gain entrance to some school. He decided to go to West Roxbury high school after we graduated from middle school. Kevin's and Rammell's moms treated me just like their son as my mother was to Kevin and Rammell. They were actually the only friends that my mother would allow me to stay with, overnight.

We were all on the same path and our mothers grew closer because of our friendship.

I already knew that Rammell and Kevin had been getting ass since we were sophomores in high school. As a matter of fact, Kevin got his first piece when we were in middle school. We had a party for Halloween and this former student visited the school for some odd reason. She was a heavy girl, but was pretty as hell. To a horny teenager like Kevin and a few other students, she was Halle Berry. This girl was also freaky as hell. It was a time when grinding on a girl to "Atomic Dog" had just started. While most of us were doing the "Wopp," this girl was going around sticking her ass up to all the horny teens and allowing them to grind on her. Some people took it a step further than grinding, and Kevin was one of those people. Rumor has it that Kevin was caught in one of the classrooms in the basement with "Big Freaky," but he has never admitted to it. I'll even admit that I copped a feel or two from "Big Freaky." Those gigantic breasts on a fifteen year-old girl was not common back then.

Rammell, on the hand, was just as slick. Also, as an only child, Rammell took advantage of the situation. His mom worked long hours while he stayed home with his senile grandmother. I caught him slipping the tongue to "Big Freaky" in the back hallway away from everybody. He was also grinding on her, humping her like they were having sex. To this day, he still denies that he had ever kissed "Big Freaky." For some reason, Big Freaky would only allow me to cop a feel. I probably would've tried to get more if she allowed it. She wasn't into me like that, but she liked Rammell and Kevin.

By the time we entered high school, my boys had become more than sexually active. Kevin was the smoothest one of the three of us. He had girls jocking him because he wore jewelry along with the latest fashion and sneakers. He got his hair cut every Friday. He was always looking fresh. My uncle may have bought me clothes, but I didn't get the expensive stuff that Kevin wore. Levi's and Lee jeans were the only types of jeans my uncle would buy me, while Kevin's mom spent money on Calvin Klein, Guess, Jordache, and Gasoline Jeans. Rammell was the least fortunate of the three of us, but he never complained because he knew how hard his mother worked to help him get the things he needed. Kevin had an older half sister on his father's side named Marsha. She was fine as hell, but she only came by occasionally to see him. Kevin also had a younger brother that he had to look after and that was why his mother spoiled him so much. It was her way of paying him for watching his brother. I can't say that Kevin's mom was struggling, because she received child support from Kevin's father who was a firefighter and her younger son's father who was a Boston Police officer. My mother was the only person who really knew how much child support Kevin's mom received because she had to provide proof of income when she was trying to rent her apartment from my mother. I heard she was getting close to fifteen hundred dollars a month in child support between her two baby daddies. Unfortunately, one of the two fathers was bitter and spent very little time with his son. Kevin's father ended up having to play the role of father to both boys.

Rammell was the horniest of the crew and he made the best of his situation by bringing home as many young girls from Latin Academy and other high schools as he could after school. He lived in a single-family house with his mother and senile grandmother. His grandmother's room was on the first floor while his room was all the way up in the attic. She couldn't walk up the stairs to bother him when he brought company over, and he always had his music loud to draw out any noise coming from his room. Rammell used to brag daily about his conquests and made us feel bad for not having as many women as him. Of course, I kept the fact that I was a virgin from both of my friends. We talked about how great of an experience it would be if any of us ever got with Ms. Charles. Kevin wasn't too much into Ms. Charles because he thought she was old. However, Rammell used to come over my house sometimes just so he could see Ms. Charles. Now that I had something up on him, I was debating whether it was worth me using it against him or not. I knew that Rammell wouldn't believe that I slept with Ms. Charles and he would try to do everything in his power to try to confirm the truth, and that was why I couldn't tell him. I also had to be careful to make sure that Kevin never saw me coming out of Ms. Charles' apartment. My friends thought I was a virgin because I never talked about any girl that I bagged, but I never confirmed it even after we graduated from high school. That was the hardest thing to do because I wanted them to know that I was getting high quality pussy while they were still messing with low-grade chickenheads.

Too Obvious

Keeping my secret from Rammell and Kevin was one thing, but there was no way I could go on without telling my uncle. As usual, my uncle came by to pick me up for a Red Sox game the Friday after I slept with Ms. Charles. "Something is different about you, boy," he said. I was grinning from ear to ear and it was a little too obvious to my uncle. "I don't know what you're talking about," I told him. "Well, anyway I'm really proud of you, Junior. You're about to graduate from one of the best high schools in the state and you're going to a prestigious university at Brown," he said. I wasn't even listening to my uncle's praise as I was lost in thought about Ms. Charles. I couldn't wait to get a piece of that ass again. My uncle turned to see that my eyes were lost in the distance and said, "I know what it is. I smell pussy on you! You got some pussy from somebody and you can't stop thinking about it." His guess was so right and I had no idea how he did it. I could only smile after he made his statement. "So who was it, Junior?" he asked. "A gentleman never tells," I responded with a chuckle. "Boy, you better tell me who gave you some pussy or you won't be getting that car that I was planning to get you as a graduation gift," he said. I had no idea that my uncle was planning on getting me a car as a gift.

I had just found out earlier in the week that I was getting a full academic scholarship to Brown University in Providence, Rhode Island and I knew that my mother had told everyone in the family about it. That must've been the reason why my uncle offered to get me a car. He had initially planned on helping me with my tuition, but he found a way to still help me because tuition was no longer a concern. So my excitement switched from pussy to driving. "You're getting me a car!" I said excitedly. "Why do you think I've been picking you up every Saturday to teach you how to drive?" he said. "I thought you just wanted me to have my license, but you're the man, Uncle Joe," I told him. "Stop getting so excited and tell me who gave you some pussy this week," he said. "You can't say anything," I told him. "Who was it?" he asked impatiently. "It was Ms. Charles," I revealed. "Boy, don't be looking all pussy whipped like the whole world can smell pussy on your breath. That's just the beginning. Now, what you need to do is learn how to become the best lover for the next few months before you go on to college," he said. "You need to be hitting that as much as you can everyday so by the time you get to college you won't be fazed by some of these hot girls, but you can't be whipped by the pussy. You have to take care of the pussy," my uncle schooled.

My uncle was a trip. We talked about what I needed to do to Ms. Charles during the entire game as we watched the Red Sox put a spanking on the Yankees. My uncle hated the Yankees and he would only go to a game when the Sox played the Yankees. "I'm proud of you, Junior. You've done everything the way I taught you and you're on your way to become one of the best lawyers in the country," he told me. My uncle and I discussed my many different interests and law was a top priority. I definitely wanted to minor in black studies as I had planned to major in political science at Brown University. My goal was to go and get it done as quickly as possible and graduate with a 4.0 grade average so I could apply to Harvard law school.

I managed to reveal my secret only to my uncle during that summer. Rammell and Kevin were definitely hitting numbers, but I'm not sure if they had the quality of pussy that I was getting. Ms. Charles became my good habit as I tried as much as I could to rush home everyday from my summer job at the bank. She and I spent a lot of time together and I was hitting it on a regular basis. My skills improved tremendously as I learned how to please Ms. Charles by making her cum at will. She especially liked my oral skills. Her pussy tasted so good, I didn't mind eating her for hours. I also felt that she enjoyed the fact that my dick would stay hard for hours at a time even after I busted three or four nuts. Ms. Charles definitely deserved the credit for making the lover that I am today.

That summer, I spent very little time with Rammell and Kevin as they were too busy trying to sleep with as many women as possible before Rammell left for Williams College in the Berkshires. Kevin decided to attend University of Massachusetts at Lowell. Rammell received a full academic scholarship. His mother was very proud of him. He had planned to study psychology, because he wanted to become a psychiatrist. Kevin was just happy to be accepted into college. He wasn't too much into his academics. Rammell tried to get me to go out on many double dates with him, but I was not interested in going out and spending money on young girls when I had mature pussy for free right below me. He and Kevin spent most of their summer job earnings on the girls that they hung out with. By the time they were leaving for school, they were both complaining that they didn't have enough money to last them through the semester. I saved every single dime that I earned and Ms. Charles even offered to send me money whenever I needed it, but I refused her offer because she was a single mother of two children. Between my uncle and my mother, I knew that I would be fine.

An Awkward Situation

Since I didn't have too many friends in high school, my mother decided to have a dinner party for my high school graduation. I was told that I could invite anybody that I wanted to, so I invited Rammell, Kevin and of course Ms. Charles and her children. My uncle was also present, which brought the tantamount of tension to an all time high. I didn't want Ms. Charles to feel uncomfortable, so I kept my conversation brief at the dinner table. I was hoping that Uncle Joe wouldn't open a can of worms that needed to be kept sealed. He showed a great amount of respect by making the evening all about me. "I've always known that you were bright and I know that you will reach peaks higher than anyone in this family has, including me," he said in a congratulatory way. "Thanks Uncle Joe. You've been my inspiration and the best role model that I've ever had. I appreciate and love my mother, but you have been the male figure that I have needed my throughout life. "That's awfully kind of you, Junior. You're the best nephew that I could ever ask for, and I'm very proud of you," Uncle Joe affirmed.

Ms. Charles was wearing a sexy pair of blue jeans with a white shirt and a black pair of pumps. She was looking great and her children looked nice in their outfits. I could almost undress her with my eyes and she could sense it. I stayed composed long enough to avoid making it too obvious to my mother and the other family members who were present. I caught my Uncle Joe glancing at Ms. Charles as if he regretted not getting with her. She was sexy as hell and her sexiness got the best of me at the table. While I sat there daydreaming about having her nipples in my mouth and my hands wrapped around her silky skin under the sheets, I developed an erection. It was at that moment that my mother decided to ask me to address the family. It was then that I realized that being well endowed was not always a good thing. I would've embarrassed myself if I had gotten up to address my family the way my mom intended me to. "Mom, I really don't have much to say," I said to her as I tried to squirm my way out of it. "Junior, you have a lot of people in this room that are proud of you and I think you at least owe them this much," my mother said. There was no way I could say no to my mother. So with my hands in my pocket trying to keep my hard dick from sight, I got up and thanked everyone for their support and for always believing in me and I promised not to disappoint any of them when I go away to college.

I was relieved that my mother didn't ask me to take my hands out of my pocket, but Ms. Charles knew why they were in there. She occasionally looked my way inconspicuously to let me know that I was on her mind as well. I knew that my uncle was laughing inside because he could see that I was pussy whipped and Ms. Charles was enamored by my innocence. I would not stay innocent for too long because Ms. Charles had planned to enjoy my company as much as possible during the summer before I left for school.

After opening my gifts, I thanked everyone again. Most of my family members gave me money as gifts. However, Ms. Charles bought me a sweater. It was a beautiful wool sweater that I could wear during the fierce winter months in New England. It was a thoughtful gesture and I knew she took her time picking it out. I also felt it was her way to make sure that she stayed on my mind while I was away at school. I went to hug her, but she inadvertently kissed me as she tried to turn her face the opposite direction from mine to hug me. There was silence in the room for a quick moment, but the kiss looked accidental because we didn't lock lips.

Everyone cleared the house by 9 o'clock that night and my fever for Ms. Charles was still going strong. I wanted to get a taste of her and I could tell from the look in her eyes that she was thirsty for me as well. Figuring out a way to get with her was my next task. Since it was little bit late, I couldn't tell my mother that I wanted to go anywhere, but my uncle would be more than willing to drive me wherever I needed to go, so I had to be slick. The street we lived on wasn't a bad street, but from Morton Street up to Selden Street, there was no telling what could happen to someone walking that way after dark. I decided to ask my uncle to drop Rammell home and I offered to tag along. I acted like I wanted to make sure he got home safe. Rammell also welcomed the chance to ride in my uncle's convertible. When I got to Rammell's house I called my mother to tell her that I would be spending a couple of hours there with him until his mother got home, at which time she would drop me home. My mother wasn't the type to keep checking up on me for no reason. She expected me home by 11:30PM and that gave me a good hour and half to be with Ms. Charles. My uncle already knew the deal, so he dropped me back at the house without letting my mother know. I snuck through the front door and knocked lightly on Ms. Charles' door. By then, her children were asleep and I knew we had to keep everything quiet.

Put It On Me

I had been salivating all night over this woman and there she was standing before me still wearing those tightly fitted, sexy jeans that I wanted to get in between with force. "Wow," was what went through my mind, as I looked at her silky-smooth skin, curvaceous body and beautiful face. I think my dick was hard from the time I set foot in her apartment, and she could see it too. She led me to her bedroom where she proceeded to turn her night radio on so the kids wouldn't hear us, in case they got up. At five and seven years old, Ms. Charles understood that her children were very curious, so she made sure her door was locked and secured. With the door secured, I felt the liberty to pull her towards me for a wet kiss. I was almost a little too voracious as I took her tongue into my mouth to savor her taste buds. Her tongue was warm and smooth and I could feel the passion rising in her as she held on to my back while we continued to kiss and take little steps towards the bed. "I've wanted you all day," she managed to whisper as she hurriedly tried to unbutton her blouse. My task was a little easier as I pulled my shirt over my head impatiently to reveal my skinny, but defined chest. The two hundred push-ups that I had been doing daily were finally paying off.

I could not anticipate what her next move would be, so I stood there looking dumbfounded with my hands intertwined together on the back of my head. Ms. Charles started licking her way down past my navel and I knew that a treat was coming. I quickly dropped my pants to the floor to reveal my hardened dick to her. She reached out and grabbed my dick with both hands. The warmth of her hands was enough to make me bust a nut right there, but I fought it. She started jerking me back and forth with one hand while caressing the tip of my dick with the other. I was trying my best not to bust in her eye as her face was relatively close to my penis. I wanted to tell her, "Put it in your mouth already," but I had too much respect for Ms. Charles. She was the one leading me to the promise land. I stood back and allowed her to take control of the situation. After stroking my dick while massaging my nuts for about two minutes, I could no longer help it. I closed my eyes and allowed my semen to exit my body freely. Ms. Charles must've been anticipating my next move, because she quickly moved back while still holding my dick in her hand to squeeze every ounce of sperm from it with a grin on her face.

Now it was my turn to make her reach for the sky. At 17 years old, fingering a woman brought some kind of abnormal pleasure to a teenager. My fingers were the best sexual tools I owned beside my dick. I had no idea that my tongue was supposed to be running a close second. I started kissing Ms. Charles again while apprehensively easing my hand down to her crotch to finger her. To my surprise, she welcomed it and I continued to stick my middle finger in and out of her pussy. She was grinding and moaning. After a while, she placed her hand over mine to motion the speed of my finger inside her. "I like this," I thought to myself. I stuck another finger inside her and she continued to grind even more. My index and middle fingers must have been doing a great job. I finger fucked her until my hand hurt and Ms. Charles was enjoying every minute of it. It was finally time for penetration. Ms. Charles handed me a condom as she lay in the bed on her back. I wasn't too much into the different positions yet, so missionary was good enough for me. To be quite honest, the sight of a pussy was good enough for me no matter what the position was. This time I knew my way to the hole, but I tried ramming my dick in her pussy. "Ease up," said Ms. Charles. I slowed it down and penetrated her wet pussy slowly as she wished. Not sure if I should hump her slow or fast, however my dick was eager to devour her pussy. I kept the same pace for about two minutes until she directed me to move faster. "I want you to fuck me harder," she commanded. It was on then. I increased the speed of my strokes and Ms. Charles started shaking while her legs were wrapped around my waist. She left no space between us, as she started winding and grinding harder to my strokes. "Oh shit! I'm coming!" she exclaimed. I had no idea what I did, but Ms. Charles came for the longest time and her body kept shaking and shaking. I came too, but not the way she did.

I was still in dreamland after Ms. Charles and I went at it for another round before I finally made my way upstairs. I would've stayed a little longer for one more round, but Ma Dukes wasn't playing and I damn sure didn't want to cut off my pussy supply. Ms. Charles was also understanding of my situation, but she told me she would like to wake up with me one day. I thought about what she said and how great it would be to spend a whole night with her, but it would be a while before that happened. I needed to focus on getting myself ready for college.

College Life

I was seventeen years old when I arrived at Brown University in Providence, Rhode Island. My future looked bright and I was excited about a new beginning. During the first two days, I attended the mandatory freshmen orientation and I got to learn my way around campus pretty well. I was housed at the Bronson house along with 450 other freshmen. My roommate was an interesting fellow from Billerica, Massachusetts. His father was a high school teacher in Boston, so he was pretty cool for a white boy. He was also a DJ and a Hip Hop enthusiast. His name was Scott De Palma but everyone called him Scotty. I was happy to have a roommate that shared my taste in music and he also understood my urban lifestyle. My only disappointment was the fact that I couldn't bring a car on campus as a freshman. I had to wait until the following year to get the car my uncle promised me.

We didn't do too much during the first couple of days of school. Scotty and I would meet up for lunch and dinner in between classes. When we had down time, we'd go to the game room to shoot pool. Scotty was also the ultimate player who was into more brown sugar than Robert De Niro. The funny thing was that the sisters gave Scotty just as much play. While I tried my best to stay focused on school, as my uncle told me before I left, I knew it would be hard because there were so many beautiful, intelligent sisters on campus. By then, I was a scrawny six-foot two inches tall, smooth skin and what most women on campus referred to as "cute." I was okay with that as long as they didn't think I was ugly. I tried as much as I could to look neat everyday and I kept to myself a lot. I also attended meetings with The African Student Association and other minority groups on campus. I met some of the brightest African American minds eager to change the world after receiving their degrees from Brown. It felt great to be among a different group of people who were respected for their minds. I felt right at home because I didn't have to pretend that I was smart. We all knew that we were at Brown because of our great minds. Back home, I had a hard time with some of my peers because they couldn't understand why I wanted to become something more than just a blue collar worker, thug or vagrant. I felt refreshed at Brown.

Scotty and I spent the first week of school familiarizing ourselves with the campus and the different buildings where our classes took place. We had a lot of fun and partied our asses off. During that time, Scotty must've banged at least three freshmen chicks who were just too eager to give it up to a white boy. It was obvious that these sisters were raised a little different than I was because their dialect was a lot more on the Caucasian side. One of the baddest sisters that I had ever seen was this mixed chick named Molly. She looked so good, I have yet to see an actress, black or white, who could stand up to her beauty. She didn't seem too comfortable around me, but she loved herself some Scotty. As time passed during the week, her beauty started to fade to me because she would come to the room at night just to give Scotty a blowjob and he treated her like shit. I almost hated that chick for allowing herself to be treated like a piece of meat by Scotty, but I wasn't mad at Scotty because he treated all the women the same. He had white chicks too, but he was more into the sistas.

"The real work starts today, I gotta start leaving these chicks alone if I wanna get the hell outta here in four years," Scotty said to me, as we were getting ready to head to class. "I think you got enough ass last week to last you through the semester," I told him. "Don't even try to make me look like a player. I saw how you were looking at Molly. You wanted a piece of that ass. She's a fine chick, but I don't like the light skinned black chicks. I like the darker chicks. You can have her," he said to me. Only if he knew that women like Molly only feel important when they allow white boys to bang them. She was not interested in a brother like me, and neither was I in her. "Nah, I'll pass. I need to stay focused so I can get the hell outta here in 4 years like you said," I said sarcastically. "Bro, I hope you're not gonna be so much into your books that you won't go pussy hunting with me sometimes?" Scotty questioned. "Pussy hunting? What the hell is that?" I asked. "When we go out to parties to find girls that we can bring back to the room with us to fuck...You do plan on fucking a few of these fine sisters on campus, don't you?" he asked. I hated the way he was talking about black women. I almost felt like punching him across his mouth, but I remained calm. "I gotta head to class. I'll see ya later," I said while walking out the door. "Are we meeting for lunch?" Scotty screamed down the hall. "No!" I screamed back.

I don't know why I was mad at Scotty. He was just being a normal, horny teenager. The fact that his skin was white shouldn't have been a problem, but it was. Rammell did the same thing all the time and I never got mad at him. I realized that I was gonna have to check myself in order to develop the proper "roommate relationship" with Scotty.

Crystal

My intentions may have been to keep my focus on my studies, but after meeting Crystal Young, my attention span seemed to have shortened in class. I found myself drifting and daydreaming about her all day, and even in class, sometimes. She was the finest sista that I had ever met up until that point in my life. She had shoulder length hair, medium brown skin, perfect pear size C-cup breasts and a derriere so round and nice. I couldn't fathom the perfect make-up of this woman. Crystal was also a freshman from Brooklyn, New York. She grew up in do or die Bed-Stuy, better known as Bedford-Stuyvesant. She had that around the way girl attitude with the intelligence and outspokenness of Angela Davis. I remember the first time I laid eyes on her; she walked through the door at the African Student Association meeting wearing what looked like a head wrap for a top and a pair of tightly fitted jeans that made all the brothers gush over her for about a minute before they refocused on what they were doing.

After she flashed her beautiful smile while introducing herself to the group, I knew that I had to have her. The good thing about being on an Ivy League campus is that you don't have to question anyone's intelligence. Crystal had only gotten into Brown because one thing and one thing only, she was smart. Her articulation only confirmed her intelligence. "Hello, my name is Crystal. I'm from Brooklyn, New York. I grew up in Bed-Stuy and I plan on studying journalism. I don't have a boyfriend and I'm not looking for one," she said surprisingly with a Brooklyn attitude. She might've thrown a hatchet in some of the guys' game plan, but I was not convinced. I was thinking to myself that she was full of herself because no one even suggested any interest in her.

The meeting lasted for about an hour and a half. Afterwards, people stood around to network while taking in some of the refreshments and cookies that were neatly laid out on the table. Crystal seemed a little standoffish to most of the people at the meeting, but I found it to be very attractive. She wasn't looking at anyone in particular when I walked up to her to introduce myself. "Hello, I'm Dave. David Richardson from Boston, Mass., but people call me Junior," I said trying to emulate her Brooklyn accent and attitude. She smiled then extended her hand to me, "I'm Crystal." "I know," I said with a grin. "Did you enjoy the meeting?" I asked. "It was a good start. I hope we can get a few things accomplished on campus. I'm a doer and not a talker," she told me. She was referring to the agenda that was discussed at the meeting. There was going to be a new cabinet elected to run the African Student Association and to make sure the black voice was heard on campus as well as organize different events to ease the transition for the black students on campus. Crystal seemed to be very interested in getting involved.

"Do you plan on seeking any of the available posts?" I asked her. "None of these people know me. They'll probably elect folks that they're already familiar with. I'm just a freshman," she said. "I wouldn't take it like that. The election is not for another three weeks. You have plenty of time to allow people to get to know you and for you to get to know them. You never know what might happen," I said encouragingly. Crystal smiled. "What time are you going to dinner?" I inquired. "Probably 6:30," she answered. "Can I meet you in the caf?" I asked. "Sure," she said. It was confirmed that we were going to meet in the cafeteria for dinner. That was one of the great things of being on campus, dinner took place at the cafeteria and no one had to pay for anything because the meal plan covered all that. The only thing I needed was great conversation.

I had to blow Scotty off, but not because of our earlier squabble. I needed to have dinner alone with Crystal. I wanted to get to know her. I left a note on Scotty's desk telling him that I would be in the cafeteria with Crystal and if he wanted to stop by to introduce himself it was okay. However, he couldn't stay. Crystal and I were getting along great during dinner until Scotty felt the need to make himself known. "Wow! You are as fine as they come," he said after reaching our table. Crystal looked him up and down and wondered who this crazy white boy was. "This is my roommate, Scotty" "And you are one sexy glass of chocolate," Scotty interrupted as he reached for her hand and planted a kiss on the back of it. "Alright Romeo, you can get outta here now," I said to him. "You're a lucky man, Dave. A lucky man," he said as he made his way to another table where a bunch of sisters were sitting. "Your roommate is a trip, but he's a cool ass white boy, though," said Crystal. "Never mind my roommate. Where were we?" I said, trying to change the subject. "Oh yes, we were talking about how you want to change the world for women and how you were gonna be sweet, kind and generous to me," I said with a little too much enthusiasm. "You're cool. I wouldn't mind hanging out with you sometimes," she said.

After dinner, Crystal and I walked back to my dorm. I wanted to show her my room, which was something that most people on campus did. I wasn't trying to bust a move or nothing, but I wouldn't turn her down if she wanted to give me some. We sat in my room for a little while and Crystal and I got to know each other a little better. She spent all of her life in Bedstuy, living in a two-bedroom apartment with her mother and her younger sister. Crystal was the first person in her family to go to college. She was class president at her high school and she got lucky when Brown University offered her a full academic scholarship. Crystal had one plan and one plan only, to graduate from Brown with honors so she could attend Columbia University to pursue a master's degree in journalism. Her goal was to become a writer with the New York Times. She was very ambitious and I admired that about her. Though we weren't trying to impress each other, I believe we were both excited about the possibilities. Crystal was trying to clown me about the way the room was set up. Scotty and I divided the room with the furniture so we can both have privacy in case we had company. We also had a curtain that divided the room in order to make our guest feel comfortable. I hadn't brought anybody to the room yet, but Scotty was enjoying the other half of the room, most nights.

We left my room after an hour to walk Crystal to her room, which was located downstairs from me. She said nothing the whole time. I was thinking she lived across campus, but she lived one floor below me. "Why didn't you tell me that you lived downstairs from me?" I asked. "I didn't know if you were gonna be a creep or not, so I didn't want to reveal too much information. But since you're cool and all, I guess it's okay for you to visit me every now and then," she said, smiling. While my room was typical, with posters of my favorite player at the time, Michael Jordan, and a couple of singers like Janet Jackson and Mary J. Blige, Crystal's room was a little more elaborate. She decorated the room with drapes and sheets and she designed a canopy over her bed on the ceiling and the smell of incense permeated the room. It was sensual and welcoming. I wanted to jump her bones right there, but I could tell that Crystal was not that kind of woman. I was gonna have to put in a little work before I got anything from her. We chilled for another hour before I decided to head back to my room, so I could get some work done. Crystal also ended up winning the treasury post after she decided to run for the available position as a freshman.

Uncle Joe

I was in my room for less than an hour doing my work when my phone rang. "Hello. What's up, Uncle Joe?" I said excitedly through the receiver. "How ya doing, Junior? Have you adjusted to campus life yet?" he asked. "I'm doing fine and I'm trying to acclimate myself to this environment, which is oh, so good," I said with a laugh in my voice. "It sounds like you're enjoying it. Just make sure you stay focused and don't get derailed by pussy. I'm not saying not to enjoy yourself, but don't get all caught up in some pussy where you'll end up flunking out of school. I was just calling to see if you need anything," he said, switching the conversation with his last statement. "Uncle Joe, I'm good for now. I already told you that I won't disappoint you or the family. You have nothing to worry about." Hindsight is 20/20 and I wish I knew then about my situation because I would've never told my uncle that I wouldn't disappoint the family. That's another story that I will talk about a little later. It had been a week since I met Crystal and she was starting to affect me even more. We even shared kisses on a few occasions, but nothing too heavy. I was trying my best to keep my uncle from detecting her breath on mine over the phone. He was good like that.

"Have you met any fine young thangs on campus yet? I know there's plenty of them on campus. The Ivy League chicks are a lot more open-minded than people think, and they're some freaks. Just be careful, Junior," my uncle warned. All I heard was the last part of his statement and all I could think about was freaking Crystal. She was gonna get it. "Junior, did you hear me talking to you?" my uncle screamed on the phone. I was snapped back into reality by his voice. "Yes, I heard you. I ain't tryna get serious with any girls right now," I lied. There really was no reason to lie to my uncle, but I needed him to feel good about my promise to finish school.

My uncle had always been there for me, and he was a lot to live up to. I started to second- guess myself wondering if I could achieve all that he wanted me to. He was so proud of his nephew, but more importantly proud of the job that he had done to help raise me. Back then, I would've given anything to become the man he wanted me to be. I already knew how proud my mother was of me, but Uncle Joe hated my father and he wanted to show him that his absence wasn't going to affect my success in life. Uncle Joe and I talked for another ten minutes or so on the phone before we hung up.

The pressure was on and I needed to make sure that I excelled at school. All my life, I had never failed at anything, and I was certain that I would walk out of Brown University summa cum laude in four years.

The Carefree Life

While most African American students don't share my experience in college, I was fortunate that my mother and uncle afforded me the ability to stay focused on my studies without having to take on an additional part-time job while I worked my 10-hr a week work-study job. It appeared as if that luxury was reserved for the white students. They walked around campus without a care in the world while driving their convertible BMW's, Mercedes, Volkswagens and Saabs. I was fortunate to get a promise of a Honda Civic courtesy of my uncle. Though it would be used, a couple of years old, I knew I would have a car, which was more I could say for most of the other black students on campus. My work-study job helped keep money in my pocket and the occasional money that I received from my mother and uncle kept me afloat for the most part when I wanted an occasional splurge. I didn't really need anything and I didn't waste money. Crystal and I occasionally went to the movies taking turns paying for each other. Going Dutch was the norm for college students on my campus. There may have been a few Black students on campus who came from money, but they didn't come around too much. Some of them seemed to have fit better with the white kids because they grew up in the suburbs their entire lives. I couldn't blame them for that. I was straight up hood from Mattapan and most of the people I knew on campus grew up in the hood as well, except for my roommate Scotty, who wished he grew up in the hood.

It's funny how people always wish for things that they have no idea about. Some black folks wish they were rich, while some white folks wish they were from the street or the hood. Some of them want to be black altogether, and some black folks want to be white without knowing how a white person lives. I was paying close attention to folks on campus. Most of the black and Hispanic folks sat together during breakfast, lunch and dinner. The self-segregation was more of a way to embrace their shared background and to form a solid front. It wasn't that we were prejudice, but the very few of us on campus needed each other for support.

It was also the most carefree period in my life as I left all the baggage associated with living on W. Selden Street back in Boston. At night, I didn't fear that someone might stick me up as I made my way to my dorm. Not that crime didn't take place on campus, but I felt a little safer because white folks supposedly make us feel safer when there's more of them present. The same crimes that happen in the hood took place on campus as well, as I later found out. Women were raped, people got mugged, cars got stolen, people fought and the police were involved, just like the hood. For whatever reason, I was carefree and I enjoyed it.

I almost felt privileged compared to some of my peers. I had friends who worried daily about their grants and financial packages, and whether or not they would be able to stay in school. Some of them had the burden of their families riding on their shoulders. I was burdened more with success than having to pull my family out of the projects. I felt bad for some of my friends because I knew that they had to work twice as hard because of all their worries. I was lucky.

Doing Ms. Thang

A couple of months had gone by and Crystal and I had been kicking it hard. She made it clear from the beginning that she didn't want a boyfriend and she was adamant about it. I figured I'd get in where I fit in, so I was trying to become her booty call. We had had some heavy petting in the past months and it was time for me, not us, to take it to the next level. I was tired of Crystal leaving me with a rock hard dick in my room every night. I decided to take the initiative of making my skills known to her this particular weekend, when Scotty went home. All semester he had not gone home once, and Crystal's roommate acted like she wanted to stay away from home to be a slut. She fucked more men on campus than Heather Hunter. She was a total and complete slut because she had a man in her bed every time I walked in with Crystal. It wasn't like I caught a break with Scotty, either. He was fucking more women than I cared to know about. He was a man whore. Crystal was always too shy to go too far with me when Scotty was on the other side of the room. However, Scotty could care less who was around as he got his knob slobbed on a regular basis with me on the other side of the curtain. Finally, Crystal and I had a weekend to ourselves in the room. The first night was the most memorable.

Everything started so innocently that night. We were kissing and then my hands found their way to her plump ass. The kissing continued as I pulled my sweater over my head to expose my bare chest. She ran her hands across my chest while sitting on the edge of the single bed. She made her way towards my belt and started unfastening it. Crystal had never been so bold in the past. The anticipation of her beautiful lips wrapped around my dick added to my ambivalence to be patient, so I rushed and helped her. The shaft of my dick was already sticking up out of my boxers by the time my pants fell to the ground at my easing. A soft kiss on my stomach followed, and I knew exactly where her lips were headed. As she rolled her tongue around her lips, I reached down to kiss her once more, still hoping there won't be a detour. Our tongue met and I grabbed the back of her head for more affect as I was trying to display the passion within me. "Ooh," she moaned after I released her from the kiss. Her moans were the greatest factor to my excitement at this time and she knew it. Still praying for a southern visit from her tongue, I silently said a quick and efficient prayer to God, "Dear God, I just want a blowjob." While her hands ran up to my chest, her tongue found its way to the head of my penis and I could hear heaven calling me. Trying my best not to succumb to the warm comfort of her tongue, I eased my body back just enough to allow her to tease me. Her hands were now on my butt as she pulled my underwear off while my dick was in her mouth. "Your dick tastes so good," she whispered. I said nothing back as my mind went numb while I relished in the moment. I never knew that Crystal had it in her, but I was ready to see all that she had.

I needed comfort, so I reached out and palmed one of her breasts as she melted me in her mouth. Her tongue strokes were nothing short of extraordinary. As my fingers stay glued to her nipples, she brought her right hand down and wrapped it around my dick while she took small licks from my giant lollipop. Stroking my dick back and forth while her lips were wrapped tight around it caused me to fumble, and there was no recovering. I grabbed the back of her head as I humped her mouth slowly. I could feel the strength leaving my body as she took a couple of ounces of my protein down her throat in a satisfying way. She swallowed. I was surprised. I thought to myself, *New York chicks are hot.* I didn't think a woman her age would allow me to cum in her mouth. "I'm sorry. I didn't mean to cum so quickly," I said to her. "It's okay," she tried to comfort me. "It's just that I've wanted you for so long…" "Say no more," she said like a mature woman. At seventeen and a half years old, no recovery period was necessary as my dick stood hard and erected and ready for more, but I wanted a little more of her as well. I needed to make her cum just as quickly as I did. I had eaten Ms. Charles enough times to know how to satisfy a woman.

I started feeling uncomfortable after cumming so quickly while she gave me the blowjob of my life, so I said to her, "Crystal, I wanna eat you. I wanna make you cum just like you made me cum." She smiled and her smile gave me the confidence to ease my way down to her breasts, taking her nipples into my mouth, sucking them gently alternating between left and right while she coyly whispered, "I like that, Junior." I knew her breasts were one of her sensitive spots because she would always tell me how wet she got when I sucked on them. I also knew if I sucked and licked them just right I could possibly get an orgasm out of her. I slowly pressed my tongue against her left nipple as it went in a circular motion while my right hand fondled her right breast. The moaning increased and I could tell that my technique was working. Switching from left to right and right to left and my index finger inside her, I was able to bring Crystal's body to a convulsion as she whispered to me, "You did it. I'm coming. Don't stop." With my ego satisfied, I wanted to taste her. It was the first time that I had made a woman cum while sucking her breasts and fingering her. She had the best smelling pussy that I had ever been in, even to this day, long after I have been in many of them, Crystal's pussy will always remain the sweetest to me. I become nostalgic whenever I think of her.

The road down to Crystal's cookie jar was straight down, and my tongue formed a cool path down her belly leisurely as I aimed to explore her pink cookies. First, I parted the lips like Moses parted the red sea, and awaiting my tongue, was the sweetest, pinkest and juiciest nana that ever existed. My erected tongue slowly brushed up and down her openness, but that was not her sensitive spot. "I want you to lick up there," she said as she pointed to her clit. I was still an eater in training and I ran off course for a minute during our lovemaking sessions. A student eager to follow direction and learn, I took her majesty's directives and the tip of my tongue landed on her erected clit. Like a puppy nibbling on his mother's breast, I nibbled on her clit slowly. "Mm, Junior," she whispered. A few soft strokes of my tongue got her to speak even more, "That's it, baby. Eat me," she said. Ego intact and recovered from my earlier fumble, I proceeded to play tag with her clit. Each time my tongue brushed up and down her clit, she was it, shaking uncontrollably at my strokes and grabbing my head for comfort. "You feel so sweet eating my pussy," she said shyly. The pinkness deep inside her was also calling my name. I hardened my tongue and then started to stroke her with it. I could taste her juices in my mouth. Then I went deeper with my tongue. I wanted her to beg for penetration. By then, her legs were spread across my single bed while I performed oral surgery on her pussy. Her movements on the bed increased as I intensified the strokes of my tongue inside her pussy. "I want you inside me," she begged. Ignoring her request, I continued to fuck her with my tongue. "I don't want to cum while you tongue fuck me. I want to cum with your dick inside me," she revealed. We still had two days left to enjoy each other and I figured the more nuts, the merrier. My tongue strokes got harder and harder and Crystal couldn't help cumming all over herself. "Oh shit! I'm cumming. I'm Cumming, baby," she announced. I was tingling inside because I knew that my skills were improving each time I had sex with a woman.

I always enjoyed her rearview and I wanted nothing more than to take her from behind. While she lay on her stomach resting, trying to take a breather after climaxing a couple of times, I eased my index finger inside her. She instantly became moist and my finger penetrated her with ease. The slow rhythm of my fingers had her cooing, "Oohs and ahs." Her grinding on my finger confirmed that she wanted more and more I gave her. One finger was not enough; she needed more. With two of my fingers in Crystal's pussy, she started winding, grinding and moaning all at once. It was a Kodak moment and I wish I had a camera. Her booty was picturesque and her movement was rhythmic. Finally, I took my fingers out of her then licked them. Her sweet nectar tasted so good. I could've eaten her all night, but her pussy was now calling my dick. So hard it was. I slipped on a Trojan condom as Crystal arched her ass up for me to enter her candy shop. Too sweet, I thought. I glided my way inside slowly. She extended her hand out to me. She wanted to feel my presence. I held her hand as I stroked her slowly from the back. In and out, I went and she held on to my hands more tightly. I went in a little deeper and she tightened up her butt. Ecstasy was near as her butt hardened with each of my strokes. I wanted to beat it, not rub it. A little smack on her ass while I stroked her was just what the doctor ordered. "Smack my ass harder," she insisted. The burning desire to unleash my voracious sexual appetite on her was subdued at the sound of her voice. I couldn't go on anymore as my intolerable patience gave in and soon found myself cumming again. I eased up tight on her pussy and grinded on her like a dog was trying to take a bite out of my ass. "Oh shit!" I screamed. She followed with her own scream, I'm cumming again Junior. Go deeper." I thought I was as deep as I could get, but I managed another inch of closeness between us before releasing another half an ounce or so of semen in the Trojan condom while she screamed in pleasure.

Crystal and I went at it about twenty or more times during the weekend. At one point, I needed to put some ice on my dick because it wouldn't go down. I fucked Crystal until my dick hurt. She never once refused my magic wand.

The Best of Time

Though Crystal and I weren't a couple, I knew that I was the only guy that she was sleeping with. Many of the other guys tried to "hit it," but she would have none of it. That pussy was mine for the rest of the year. I can't say the same about my dick belonging to her. I didn't go home too often, but when I did, I was tearing up Ms. Charles, I mean Kelly's pussy like it belonged to me. I never could understand why Kelly never had a boyfriend. She had everything going for her. I felt it was too personal to ask and I also didn't want to jeopardize the gateway to free pussy when I came home.

Kelly was the primary reason Crystal became addicted to my dick at school. She made me a better lover. Every time I came home, she treated me like I had been gone for years. She would take her kids to her mother's house so that we could roam naked freely around the apartment and have sex on every piece of furniture in that apartment. Back massages were the norm and extended blowjobs became regular. Over time, I developed enough resistance to her touch, thus I was able to last a lot longer and satisfy her more. It was also easier for me to try new things with Kelly because she didn't expect me to be an expert because of my age. Whenever something didn't work for her, she taught me how to do it the right way so that I could be a better lover. The best time that I ever had with Kelly was during spring break one year.

I had a week off from school, but I decided to go away to Jamaica only for the latter part of the week from Thursday through Sunday, courtesy of my generous uncle. After making the Dean's list during the fall semester, my uncle agreed to send me to my choice of destination for spring break. While it was tempting to go away for a week to Jamaica to enjoy the sun and have fun with my peers, I found it even more alluring when Kelly offered to take a couple of days off from work to be home with me. It was the perfect opportunity for me to enjoy her completely without any interruptions. My mother was off to work early in the day and Kelly sent her kids off to school around the same time. It was as if my body was conditioned to be fully awake the minute my mother walked out the door. There was this burst of energy in me as I leaped up from the bed to jump in the shower to freshen up for Kelly. I must've brushed my teeth for fifteen minutes straight that morning making sure that tart morning taste in mouth was properly extracted so I could have the freshest breath.

I never had Kelly to myself for more than a couple of hours in the past. I wanted to enjoy her and play with her as if she were my favorite toy, all day long. Due to the brisk wind so prevalent in New England during the month of February, I could almost hear the door slam as Kelly made her way back into the building after dropping her kids off at school. I almost rushed downstairs in anticipation, but I decided to eat a bowl of cereal for energy sake and also to give Kelly time to get ready for me. I had told her the night before that I was coming downstairs the minute my mother walked out the door. My excitement couldn't be contained as I imagined all the things that I was gonna do to Kelly that morning. With every bite of my favorite Captain Crunch cereal, I rushed to get to the bottom of the bowl so I can gulp down the leftover milk. Finally, I was done. It was time for me to glide my way downstairs to the heavenly domain that awaited me. A white t-shirt, blue jeans and my fuzzy slippers were enough clothes for me to wear to Kelly's house. I stepped halfway out of the apartment and I realized how silly my fuzzy slippers looked. They were reminiscent of a child. I quickly ran back to the apartment and threw on my shell toe Adidas. Now feeling a little more mature, I was ready to let Kelly have me for the day.

"Knock, knock" went unanswered for about thirty seconds. I knocked again, three times this time. "The door is open," Kelly managed to whisper. The sexy sound of her voice ignited the fire in my pants and I just knew that I was gonna jump her bones the moment I set foot inside the house. I slowly opened the door to find Kelly standing in the middle of the hallway wearing a garter belt, high heels, a see-through bra, fishnet stockings and swinging a pair of handcuffs in her hands. Kinky, I thought. Kelly was a freak and I was about to get turned out, I believed. "I've been expecting you," she said in a low, sexy tone. Needless to say, the button on my jeans was about to pop out, because my dick was expanding by the second.   Kelly walked towards me then grabbed my hand to lead me to the bedroom. I was as obedient as ever as I followed behind her while she held my hand like a child. I wanted her to unleash whatever punishment she had in mind on me. "I don't want you to do anything because I will do everything for you and to you," she said.   That's what I called catering to her man. She lifted my arms to pull my shirt over my head. I could feel the frigid air hitting my chest as goose bumps started to develop around my body. Kelly must've kept her apartment at room temperature because she knew it was about to get hot in there.

She was soon licking my erected nipples gently as she tried to unfasten my pants. Eager to help, I reached down to unbutton my pants. She pulled my hands back up. "I got this, baby," she whispered softly. If she whispered like that once more, I was gonna bust a nut in my pants. The outline of her body absorbed my whole being. Kelly's body was probably the best body that I had ever seen for the better part of my pubescent years and early twenties. Her curves were dangerous; tiny waist, perfect breasts, flat stomach and an ass that didn't want to quit. I closed my eyes for a few minutes because the gazing from her eyes as she licked my nipples was enough to make me lose control. As she pulled my pants halfway down to my thighs, she realized that I needed to sit on the bed so she could take my shoes off. "Sit on the bed for a minute for me," she ordered politely. I leaned back on the bed thinking she was about to take my dick into her mouth. The room was completely dark as I closed my eyes again anticipating being immersed in the warmth of her mouth. "Mmmmm," I cooed thinking her warm hands were about to unravel my snake straight into her mouth. Instead, she went down to my feet and pulled my sneakers off. Still, I waited with anticipation. My body was no longer submitting to the chilly temperature of the room. My blood was boiling and my dick was reaching for the sky, standing straight up like a missile headed for space.

One by one, my sneakers came off and Kelly began to pull my pants off. She stroked my dick a little through my underwear as my pants went past my thighs and towards the floor. I was a little too eager and Kelly could sense it. "Go up on the bed a little," she told me. I went up and she reached for my hands. Before I knew it, my hands were wrapped around the headboard in silver handcuffs. "I'm gonna do you like you've never been done today," she told me. "Bring it on baby," I said happily. With my hands cuffed, my dick trying to pierce its way out of my boxers, I tried to anticipate Kelly's next move. She left the room for a second and came back with this massage oil.

She proceeded to pull off my boxers, allowing my skin to rest against the soft satin sheet. I could smell the flavored oil that she poured in her hands. As she rubbed her hands together with the oil, the strawberry scent permeated the room. I thought it to be liquorish. Up and down my thighs, she went as the liquid heat up in her hands. She ran her hands ever so gently against my thighs; it tickled a little. The ascension towards my crotch kept the blood flowing full force and my dick was at its peak. "Mm, your dick looks so delicious," she revealed as she rubbed it up and down. My eyes shuttered as her warm hands stroked me back and forth. She eased herself onto the bed as she took the head in her mouth.

Her tongue started performing a miracle as it went around the shaft of my dick. I felt like I was floating on thin air. Then she started sucking it gently with her lips wrapped tight around it. "You like that?" she asked as if she needed an answer from me. With heavenly lips like hers, an answer was not even necessary. Though Kelly was in charge of everything, I wish she would turn around and place her pussy on my face so I could lick it. She was sucking my dick while her ass was facing me and I just wanted to stick my tongue in and out of her. Finally, she rolled a condom down my dick and straddled me while facing the mirror that sat on the dresser across the bed. She held on to my knees as she allowed all of my nine and a half inches to penetrate her deeply. She started winding and grinding and I could see ecstasy in her face. Kelly liked when I was deep inside her. She didn't waste an inch as she scooped my dick up with her ass and kept it all inside her until her wetness got all over me. "Fuck this pussy, Junior," she started to hum as she neared her nut. I lifted my ass off the bed to help connect my strokes to her grind. I could feel her pussy wall against the tip of my dick. "You're hitting my spot, Junior!" she screamed. I knew it was a matter of minutes before Kelly came once more. I gave hurried strokes as her juices flowed down my thighs. She held on tight to my knees as she jerked another orgasm out of her body. "Oh shit! Yeah! Here it comes! Haaaaaaaaaa!" Kelly collapsed on my leg for a good fifteen minutes before we went at it again.

Kelly and I had sex for most of the day that day and the next and the day after that until it was time for me to leave for Jamaica. I barely had an ounce of strength left when I boarded the plane to Jamaica. My roommate was meeting me there along with a few other students at the school, and I was looking forward to hanging out with my peers. Pussy would be the last thing on my mind, I thought.

No Normalcy

Before I left for Jamaica, I thought that I had enough of Kelly to satisfy my pussy needs for a month, but boy was I wrong. I met a couple of chicks down there and I ended up screwing them the entire time I was there. My dick would not stay down and my dumb ass roommate stayed drunk and horny most of the time. However, there were two ladies that I met in Jamaica that I won't forget any time soon.

Scotty and I decided to chill at the resort where we were staying on this particular Saturday night. There was a club there and only guests from the resort were allowed to party at this club. The DJ wasn't the best that I had ever heard, but he played enough Bob Marley songs to make up for what he lacked in other areas as a DJ. I was standing around talking to Scotty when three white chicks from Oregon approached us. "Where are you guys from," they asked. I knew that Scotty's first choice was always a sista, but I needed him to take one for the team that night. "We're from Boston," we both said in unison. I quickly took inventory of the Kim Kardashian look-alike and I knew she was gonna get it. "Do you play basketball?" she asked. Why not? I figured I could be a basketball star while I was in Jamaica. Scotty jumped in before I had a chance to say anything. "You're looking at one of the top draft picks for the NBA draft next year. My man here is the top scorer in college. Do you guys watch basketball?" Scotty asked. "No." Since they didn't watch basketball, Scotty exaggerated his lies even more. By the time the girls ended up in our room, I had a one-hundred and fifty million dollar contract on the table waiting for me from the

Charlotte Bobcats. Needless to say, the biggest orgy went down that weekend.

Marcy was the finest one of the three. She was dark haired and stacked in all the right places. She had a body like she'd discovered the special pill that sisters had been taking all the years that produced a booming ass. Shorty had back. I never saw so much booty on a white girl in my life. Kirsten was a pretty blond with titties the size of watermelons, but very little ass. Her ass was so flat it could've been used as a bench. Allison was the least attractive of the three with auburn hair and straight up and down with no curves. However, she had a gorgeous smile, and she was the most aggressive.

We brought the girls back to my room. Allison decided to lead and take charge of the whole situation. Having been drunk from drinking all day as part of their all-inclusive package at the Sandy Bay resort, the girls had no boundaries. She started off with a little strip tease for me and Scotty while her friends looked. She was winding and grinding while taking her shirt off, and moments later, Kirsten joined her. I think both Scotty and I wanted to see Marcy more than any of them. We started cheering her on to join the other two girls. Kirsten's bodacious titties were all over my face by now and I was sucking on them like a baby while Scotty entertained Allison with his tongue on her navel. I was buried in Kirsten's melons when I noticed another tongue licking the same nipple that I had my tongue glued to. I knew Scotty wasn't crazy enough to do some homo shit like that, so it was a pleasant surprise when I turned to find Marcy joining in the fun and getting her thrill off sucking Kirsten's titties. I slipped my tongue into her mouth and we started kissing. Kirsten cut between us and now I had two mouths and two tongues to service.

Moments later, Scotty and Allison vacated the sofa and joined the three of us on the king size bed. "We want to see some skin," said Allison as she attempted to pull Scotty's shirt over his head. Kirsten and Marcy followed suit with me. The girls all decided to strip totally naked at once. I was looking at Marcy's tanned body and I couldn't wait to penetrate her. Allison and Kirsten were an afterthought. "We're not gonna stand here in our birthday suits while you boys still have your pants on. Drop those pants and your drawers while you're at it," said Allison, almost a little too eager to get fucked. I finally took off my pants and unleashed the snake. All three white girls were singing me praises, but I felt bad for Scotty because he was a couple of inches short. "Oh my God, you have a huge cock," said Allison. Scotty was very cocky and knew that he had a big dick for a white boy at seven inches. "What about this cock here, is anybody gonna breathe some life into it?" Scotty asked while the girls scrambled to give me a blowjob. Kirsten had the best skills and she almost made me cum prematurely, as she worked that magical tongue around my dick while using her hand to play with my nuts. I placed my hands on the back of my head when Marcy and Kirsten attacked my dick, exchanging licks like two tennis players going for love. Allison wanted some of the action, as well. She left Scotty to be pleased by Kirsten while she took post around my nine and a half inches.

"Your cock is so big, I can suck it all day," she revealed. Marcy smiled as she held it up for Allison to lick. "Kirsten, you can stay over there. I'll be over here for a while," she screamed across the room. I really wished she would make her way to Scotty for a double team so I could start fucking Marcy. My fingers were now playing tic tac toe as they connected with the ladies' pussies. I was fingering both of them simultaneously, but I really wanted Marcy. Her ass, C cup breasts and tight body had the blood flow down my dick at its maximum. I started to find Allison annoying, even. "Can I get a little double action over here?" Scotty begged. "Why don't you go over there to give Scotty a little treat while I give Marcy a little one on one attention," I said to Allison. She wasn't too happy about my suggestion, but she got up and went over to join Scotty and Kirsten anyway. I really didn't want to eat this white chick that I had just met, but Marcy's pinkness was screaming for my tongue, and her body was just too sick for me to pass that up. My tongue found its way between Marcy's legs. I started eating her pussy better than any white boy ever could. "Oh shit, I didn't think black guys could eat pussy, but you are doing a great job," Marcy said out loud for everybody to hear. The moaning and groaning from her just brought everybody to a halt as they watched my tongue action between her legs. Kirsten came back and joined us as she started sucking on Marcy's breasts while I ate her.

It was fun watching Kirsten suck on Marcy's breasts. She then joined me and started licking her clit. My dick was at its peak and I was ready to fuck the hell out of Marcy, then Kirsten and then Allison, and so I did. I slipped on a condom in no time. Kirsten was on top of Marcy, kissing her and sucking on her breasts while my dick was inside her pink slippery pussy expanding her walls. I was smacking Kirsten's flat ass while I fucked Marcy. Her pussy was nice and warm as I gave her my longest strokes. "That cock feels so good inside of me, fuck me!" she exclaimed. I could see Kirsten's clit rubbing against Marcy's clit as my dick took over her pussy. I was turned on to the umpteenth power. "Oh yes. Fuck me," she continued to scream. "I want some too," said Kirsten after listening to Marcy screaming to me to keep fucking her. I pulled my dick out of Marcy's pussy and inserted it in Kirsten's. I reached for her big breast and found a rhythm that wasn't there when I was inside of Marcy. I stroked and humped and humped and stroked Kirsten while she and Marcy locked lips. "You really know how to fuck," said Kirsten while enjoying my strokes. "I told you," confirmed Marcy. I kept fucking her hard.

Meanwhile, Scotty had Allison bent over on the couch while he fucked the hell out of her. Not much was being said, but Scotty was putting in a lot of work. Allison's gazing eyes were fixated on my dick as it went in and out of Kirsten. I wanted to fuck Marcy doggy style, so I asked Kirsten to make her way back to Scotty while Marcy got on all fours so I could take her from behind. I held on to her ass like a pony as my dick parted her pink lips into her slippery hole of pleasure. I was fueled by her round booty. I started smacking her ass lightly while I stroked her. "I want you to smack my ass harder," she said. The harder I smacked her ass, the stronger my strokes became. I wanted to fuck this chick to exhaustion. I pumped away into her pussy as she stretched one of her legs up opening her ass up for total penetration. My fingers were firm against her clit while I stroked. "I'm about to cum," she announced. I kept my strokes steady and held on to her extended leg. Marcy started to grind harder and with a few more strokes, she let it all out, "I'm coming. Oh my fucking God, I'm coming."

By then, I was satisfied and didn't really care about the other two women, but I went along and fucked Kirsten and Allison together while Scotty tried his best to get a repeat performance from Marcy, but he couldn't take her there. Allison's pussy was a little tighter and she talked the dirtiest of all the women. "Fuck me. Give me all of that big black dick," she said as she grinded on me. I found myself fucking her angrily trying to make her pay for using the words "big black dick." I stroked her hard and smacked her ass even harder. "That's it! Fuck me. Make me cum!" she yelled. My strokes became volatile as I tried to rip the inside of Allison. And finally, I gripped her legs and pushed all my nine and a half inches inside of her before she started yelling, "Yes! You're doing it. Fuck me!" I fucked and fucked until her pussy swelled up and got her to shake from a climatic trance that she had never experienced before.

Kirsten was the last one to make me exert the last ounce of energy that I had left in me. She got off on me fucking her titties. I placed my dick between her melons for a titty sandwich. With each stroke between her breasts, my dick would land in her mouth. For some reason, it did nothing for me. I was really fueled when Kirsten said, "I want you to fuck me in the ass. The baby oil lubricant served its purpose as I rubbed it on the condom wrapped around my dick before inserting it in Kirsten's ass. I was ramming her ass pretty hard and Kirsten was taking it well. "Fuck my ass," she said as I stroked her. Since her ass was flat, I had to hold on to her big titties while I stroked her. I pulled on her long blonde hair while I fucked her ass hard until she finally came. Afterwards, Marcy and Kirsten sucked my dick until I exploded in their faces. I never saw those white girls ever again. My time in Jamaica was well spent, but I would've had a better time if I had my homeboys with me. Rammell and Kevin would've had a ball in Jamaica.

After I got back to the States, it was business as usual. I went to class, had sex with Crystal, and went about my merry way everyday. My ego wanted me to believe that Crystal was hooked on me, but she never displayed any strong emotion towards me. She was aloof even. I found it rather odd. However, I enjoyed the perks that came along with dating Crystal. For some reason, far more women were interested in me because of her and even many more guys were interested in her because of me. Crystal was a natural beauty anyway, but I couldn't understand why so many other women on campus were trying to give me ass simply because she was sleeping with me. I knew that Crystal had nothing to do with that because she was as secretive as they come. She probably never told anyone on campus that I ever as much even smelled her coochie. That was fine with me, because I enjoyed privacy, which was something that was hard to come by on campus.

Crystal was the only woman on campus to ever set foot in my room. All the other women that I was messing with brought me to their rooms. I found myself drifting in class once, wondering where my next piece of ass was going to come from. That day, I realized that I needed to take hold of myself before I flunked my way out of Brown University. I needed to create some normalcy in my life. While it seemed customary for most college students to try to live it up during their first semester at school, I just couldn't do that. Too many people expected too much from me. I needed to focus on my studies and regroup. I decided that Crystal was going to be the only woman that I would sleep with for the rest of the year. I stuck to my guns and never looked at another woman on campus for that entire year. The temptation was always there, but I ignored it. Most of the time if I felt that I absolutely had to have another piece of ass, I would go home for the weekend and sneak in a nut or two with Kelly.

Kevin and Rammell didn't make things easier on me either. It seemed as if my school was their hunting ground. They were visiting me a little too often and it started to interfere with my studies. Every time these two knuckleheads visited, I ended up partying the total weekend away without opening any of my textbooks. Some people started to think that they attended my school; they were there so often. I had fun hanging out with them, but I had to put my foot down and bring everything to a halt. They couldn't visit when I had midterms, final exams or any kind of special test that I needed to pass. My boys understood how important school was to me and they honored my request. All the pussy hunting we used to do was wearing thin on me. Kevin was on the brink of flunking out of school. Kevin almost flunked every single class that semester. He didn't seem to care much because he only decided to go to college because Rammell and I decided that's what we wanted to do.

Me, Rammell and Kevin

Rammell was more like a brother to me while Kevin was like a close cousin. Whenever I talked to Kevin, our conversation always ended up being about some girls or what new pussy we should be chasing. It was starting to become a little redundant and after a while, I started ignoring his calls. He never once talked about his adjustment to college life, or how he was doing at school. Whenever I brought up his studies, he always said the same thing,"I don't really wanna talk about school right now. I'm here, aren't I?" I became very concerned because I was starting to sense that Kevin didn't really want to be in school. Through a conversation with Rammell, I found out that his mom used Rammell and me as examples of good kids to force him into school. Kevin resented the comparisons between himself and us, but he never let on. I wanted all of us to succeed and walk away with our degrees in four years, but Kevin's heart just wasn't in it.

Rammell and I often talked about how we were gonna get a fly ass apartment in the South End part of Boston after we graduated from college and how we were gonna be bachelors for life. For some reason, we never included Kevin in our plans. I don't know if we did that subconsciously, but it forced me to think about my friendship with Kevin. I had known him almost as long as I'd known Rammell, but I always maintained a certain distance with him. I knew that I enjoyed being friends with Kevin, but I never trusted his judgment. He could fly off the handle at any moment. I remember we once got into a big fight with these kids from Four Corners, a different section of Dorchester in Boston, all because Kevin needed to prove that people from our part of town were tougher. The stupid thing about the situation was that we were outnumbered almost two to one. It was Kevin, Rammell and I going against five dudes from Four Corners. This happened while we were juniors in high school.

We were standing at the bus stop at Ashmont Station waiting for the number 26 bus so we could get our asses home. And that's when the other crew showed up. They called themselves the Four Corner Click. They were walking up and down the station punking everybody in their way. We were standing there observing the scene without deciding what we would do if they targeted us. To be honest, I was shaking in my pants and hoping that I wouldn't have to fight these guys. As the one with the loudest mouth made his way towards us, Kevin stepped in his path. "Yo! We down with the Selden Crew, you might wanna watch who you bumping into," Kevin said after purposely bumping into the guy without giving us any warning. That Selden Crew shit was the reason why Kevin thought he was so tough. A bunch of malt liquor drinkers and weed smokers decided one day while getting high and drunk that they would form a crew called the Selden Crew. Whether you wanted to be part of that crew or not, if you lived in the surrounding areas you had to be down with them. They developed a notorious reputation very quickly, robbing people, beating people and doing all sorts of mischievous shit they had no business doing. Kevin reveled in the fact that he was affiliated with this crew. Rammell and I chose to stay away from this crew's activities because it only led to one path and that was jail.

Rammell and I had no choice but to stand guard with our fists balled up and ready to fight after Kevin decided to make the choice for us. The leader of the click was a little apprehensive at first, but he had to show his machismo after terrorizing half the people at the station. "Yo punk, what you gonna do?" he said to Kevin. Me and Rammell already knew the score. Kevin responded the only way he knew how. He clocked the dude with a right hand while Rammell and I took on two of his partners. We didn't have to tussle much because Kevin had knocked out two of them, which made it an even fight. After kicking their asses, one of them got up and said, "We're gonna get you motherfuckers." I didn't necessarily know how serious he was at the time, but since Boston is a small city and we had embarrassed the shit out of them, I knew they would be out for blood. The next time we'd run into these guys, I knew there would either be gun play or bloodshed.

We laughed about the situation on the bus, but Rammell and I were scared shitless. We knew how to handle ourselves, but we weren't thugs. Kevin was the most thuggish of the three of us and that was because he hung out with the older guys behind the Thompson Middle School, located up the street from our house, drinking forty-ounce malt liquor and smoking weed all night with them. It was like he had two personalities, but every now and then the personalities crossed paths. We weren't worried about Kevin because we knew he had access to guns, knives, and probably grenades, if he needed them. However, Rammell and I needed to avoid Ashmont Station at all cost. We knew these kids were gonna be waiting at Ashmont Station everyday looking for us. We found alternative ways to get home so we wouldn't run into this click again. Kevin didn't see it that way. He wanted to make sure everyone knew he represented the Selden Crew. The irony with Kevin's situation was that he clammed up around his mom. If his mom ever caught him acting tough on the streets, she would beat him silly with her purse and he would stand there without saying a word.

Kevin decided to go looking for the guys with his crew members to finish the beef and that brewed into one of the worst beefs that Boston had ever seen. Many innocent victims got stabbed because they were either part of the Selden Crew or the Four Corners Click. Most of them had nothing to do with the initial beef, but the lingering effect of the beef affected many victims who were down for their crew. Kevin continued to lead a double life as a decent student and a good kid at home, while he was a rebel on the streets. The fact that his mom worked the evening shift gave him plenty of time to hang out with his fellow gang members. Since cell phones weren't as prevalent back then, Kevin's mom used to call the house on her break from work to check up on him. Her calls were habitual and Kevin knew the timeframe to be home to receive the calls. She had no idea that her son was roaming the streets while she was hard at work. The older gang members became the father that Kevin never had, but they also understood his potential. Kevin was naturally gifted and intelligent, and the fellas recognized it right away. They protected him while still allowing him to play his little thug role on the streets. Kevin also protected me and Rammell. The gang members never messed with us because they knew Kevin was our friend. He would always stick up for us and made sure that we weren't harassed by the Selden Crew. Kevin was our only link to the street.

Moving On

My first year at Brown was a little harder than I anticipated. While I may have been top of my class back in high school, I wasn't on par with the rest of the students at Brown. I literally had to play catch-up for the entire first semester. My advanced math classes in high school served no purpose in college because the white students were far more advanced than I was. My vocabulary and writing skills seemed to have been remedial at best, but somehow I managed to graduate with honors from the Boston Public High School system. While at Brown, I realized that I never started on the same page as my classmates because they were so far ahead of me. The curriculum used in the public schools definitely was poor when compared to the suburban curriculum. I finally caught on by mid October and I started to understand what was going on. I didn't blame any of my professors because they assumed that my coursework in high school prepared me to be a student at Brown. At times, I felt like giving up and too ashamed to sign up for a tutor. However, when I realized what was at risk, my pride took a backseat as I allowed my tutor to help me get to where I needed to be in order to have a successful semester.

Life was a lot better the second semester as I breezed through my classes. I was able to maintain a 3.7 grade average and no longer needed a tutor. I kept my ass in the library as much as possible during the week and did my partying on the weekends. Crystal kept me on track, as she became my confidant and friend, in addition to my sex partner. We pushed each other whenever one of us felt the need to stop trying. I truly appreciated having her in my life during my freshman year, because there were times when I wanted to pack my things and head back home.

The first year went by without a hitch. I made many friends on campus and my popularity increased. I had far more associates by the end of my first year of college. I still considered Rammell and Kevin my only true friends because I grew up with them and we stayed close throughout our first year in college. It was like we never left Mattapan because we were always in each other's faces on the weekends. Rammell was able to maintain a 3.5 grade average during his first year at Williams, but Kevin unfortunately flunked out of school the second semester. His heart just wasn't into it and he made no effort to pass any of his classes. We went home that summer a little disappointed in Kevin because we wanted to graduate from college together and have the biggest bash in Mattapan for our graduation.

I was able to get a job with the State of Massachusetts during the summer as a (JTPA) Job Training Partnership Act monitor. I went around to different job sites established by the state for low-income youth and my job was to make sure that the participants were gaining work experience as well as developing good skills and work habits. I had to make sure that the participants signed in and out for work and lunch. I also made sure the proper work permits were in place as well as the proper supervision for each worksite. I ended up loving the job and the $12.00 an hour salary was very attractive to a broke college student like myself.

Rammell was able to land a summer job at the Bank of Boston working in their Charitable Trust Department. His duties consisted of following up with donors, filing, making copies, and opening the mail everyday. He didn't care too much for the job, but he got to earn some money and he met a lot of people like M. L Carr from the Boston Celtics and a few other notables. Kevin on the other hand was looking for a full-time job. His uncle was able to help him land a job as a driver with UPS. He knew he had to get a job because his mom had threatened to kick him out of the house if he didn't start contributing. She was upset that he left school, but she still loved her son, so she allowed him to stay with her while he helped her out with the bills.

I can't forget about Kelly. Kelly and I had the best of time that summer. I spent most of my free time with her and we got to explore each other's bodies like sand on the beach. She was always on top of me or I was exploring her shores and keeping my feet wet in her water. There was one time when I caught her walking through the double door and I had this daring feeling oozing out of me. I didn't even give her a chance to say anything as I pinned her up against the wall and shoved my tongue in her mouth. I already knew that my neighbors weren't home and my mother was not due to come back to the house until late that evening. Kelly was wearing a grey skirt, white blouse and carrying a black briefcase in her hand. All I heard was the loud thump of her briefcase hitting the floor as my fingers managed to pull her panties to the side while I held up her leg on one of my arms. She stuck her tongue deep in my mouth as my fingers invaded her wet hole. Kelly was looking sexy and hot and I wanted to have her in the hallway. Impatient, I unbuttoned her blouse and buried my mouth into her chest. Her supple nipples were a little bitter from her sweating in the hot sun, but I liked it. Silence fell on both of us as she anticipated my next move while immersing herself in my action.

I rolled up her skirt and scooped down to get a taste of her nectar. I ran my tongue across her pussy once and she said, "I like that." Though the entrance to her door was a few feet away, the excitement of taking her in the hallway took precedence. My tongue soon connected with her clit and I started eating her wildly. She had no control of the situation as she grabbed my head while my tongue whipped moans and groans out of her. Kelly had the best thighs. I licked my way between her thighs from her knee up to her crotch and then stuck my tongue inside of her. "I like that," she whispered. I can feel her juices flowing and my dick popping out of my pants. Without hesitation, I stuck my dick inside Kelly, raw, and she gasped in relief. Though she was worried about the possibility of a pregnancy, she allowed me to stroke her. Her pussy felt good and I needed relief from a long day's work. My pants were down to my knees as I continued to stroke her against the wall. "Oh shit, Junior, you feel so good but you can't cum in me," she said. I didn't plan on it. I palmed her ass and got closer to her, and took her tongue in my mouth as I continued to hump my way up her sugar wall. I could feel her knees were about to buckle underneath her, so I stood still while she grinded on my dick until she reached the sky, and I was not far behind. With a couple more I strokes, my own ecstasy was fighting its way out and I had to quickly pull out to allow my semen to spurt out, but like a good protein enthusiast, Kelly never let good semen go to waste. She wrapped her lips around my dick and took it down like her favorite milkshake. Afterwards, we went inside her house for round two.

It seemed like time went by pretty quickly that summer. One minute we were out there working during the week and having fun during the weekend. Before we knew it, it was time to pack up the car and head back to school again. I was excited about bringing a car to school my sophomore year. My uncle bought me a used Honda Civic, which was brand new to me, even though it was a couple of years old. I was so grateful. I could hardly see outside my window by the time I finished packing all my belongings into the car. My uncle also drove his car along with my mom to help bring the rest of my stuff to school. I also got lucky my sophomore year. I was able to get a single room in the dormitory.

My 2nd Year

My adjustment to college took place the first semester of my freshman year in college. By the time I arrived on campus my second year, I was the king on campus. I was familiar with everything and almost everyone. By everyone, I mean all the minority students on campus. There weren't that many of us at Brown to begin with, so we sort of all knew each other. Whenever we went to one of our parties, and it was always the same faces, we had no choice but to get acquainted. The year was set off with a "welcome back to school" party organized by the Black Student Organization on campus. This party was our chance to get a look at the fresh meat, as well as the opportunity to make the new freshmen class feel welcomed. I looked around and saw a bevy of freshmen girls looking to get a taste of college life. By bevy, I meant more new girls than the previous year. It also included the transfers from other schools. For some reason Crystal had decided that she wasn't going to return to school that year. I was a free man with no obligation to anyone.

I could see the excitement on their faces as they walked around introducing themselves to the upper classmen. Many of them looked like geeks, but I could tell that there were also some undercover freaks among them. Since I wasn't much of a dancer, I stood back and observed. As the DJ was spinning the latest tunes, I was trying to scope an easy prey. My fallback, shy-guy role worked to perfection as this young woman accosted me for a dance. I didn't precisely have two left feet, but I was not as swift as Usher on the dance floor. I was standing there taking inventory of this beauty who was light skinned, and had perfect teeth, light brown eyes, and a booming ass. She lacked in the chest department, but tits are for kids anyway, I believed. I wasn't exactly doing the two-step, but my ass was limited as she turned around to give me a good view of her round booty while grinding against my crotch. I could only stand there to enjoy the moment and allow myself to be turned on by the visuals. She bumped and grind and bumped and grind. My dick started growing by the second and the minute she felt it hard against her ass, she started grinding harder. That was inviting enough for me to start chatting with her. "What's your name?" I asked over the blaring sound coming from the speakers. "Janet. What's yours?" she asked. I saw an opening for a light moment and I couldn't help myself, "Can I call you Ms. Jackson, cause I'm nasty." She smiled and I discovered comfort on her face. "My name is Dave, but people call me Jr." "Are you a junior?" she asked. "As a matter of fact, I am. I was named after my dad," I said confidently. "I meant as in school. Are you a junior?" she asked again. I almost felt the need to lie to her ass, but I caught myself. "Nah, I'm a sophomore," I revealed truthfully. The DJ suddenly changed the music to "Doing The Butt" by EU. As if she wasn't already doing the butt against my dick. I saw this excitement on her face as she stuck her ass up in the air and started to demonstrate her winding and grinding skills. I want some of this, I said to myself.

One thing led to another and Janet somehow ended up in my room butt naked that night. Ass was looking good and my dick was ready to do work in a dampened space. Janet started playing with my dick like she had something to prove. She kept stroking my shit back and forth as if it was an enjoyable thing, but she was really hurting my dick. I sat there and took the pain as our tongue twirled for about ten minutes. She wasn't the best kisser, but it was good enough for me to want to fuck her. I started playing with her nipples while we kissed and I could tell she was game to go all the way. My fingers soon made their way down to her pussy and I started fingering her. As I eased my finger in and out of her, I suddenly inhaled this weird odor that infected the room. It was time for a closer inspection. I kissed her navel slowly and proceeded to invade her private area. The closer I got, the stronger the odor became. By now, the entire room was contaminated and there was no way she didn't smell that shit. After taking a whiff of the finger that I had just taken out of her pussy, my dick suddenly lost its wind and sailing was as good as done. "Goddamn!" I yelled out loud. "What's the matter?" she asked. "What's the matter, you don't smell that shit?" I said to her. "Smell what?" she asked confusingly. "Smell this," I took my finger and rubbed it on her nose. "What's that?" she asked trying to be stupid. "That shit is you. That's your pussy smelling like that. You need to wash your shit. Damn!" I didn't mean to embarrass her, but that shit smelled like a dead rat and she should've been jailed for walking around with her pussy stinking so bad. Needless to say, it was the last time I saw Janet. She tried as much as she could to avoid running into me the rest of year. Unfortunately, she wasn't the only woman that I encountered on campus with that problem.

I also met Sexy Brenda during my sophomore year at the university. She was a different kind of woman. She was a stallion built to rock a man's world. A beautiful dark skinned sister from Philly with enough body to drive the whole school crazy, Brenda was the shit. I met her in the cafeteria a couple of weeks after school had begun and we took to each other right away. A bit shy at first, but Brenda opened up to me very quickly. I helped get her familiar with campus and the surrounding areas. Brenda was sexy in every sense of the word. She stood at 5ft 8inches with beautiful black olive skin, a booty that could stop traffic, thick child-bearing thighs, and breasts that would make a grown man hungry. A perfect size 8 with enough muscle to put Serena Williams to shame, Brenda was the complete physical package.

I just knew that I had to have her. Her sexy strut was unavoidable. All the brothers drooled every time she set foot in the cafeteria. Brenda was always alone and she sat by herself at dinner everyday. One day I mustered enough courage just to say a simple "hi." Her beauty was intoxicating and intimidating. It took a lot of confidence on my part to even approach her, while all the other cowards were wishing that she would shut me down. Over time, Brenda revealed to me her harsh upbringing in foster homes, and how she felt herself "lucky" to be able to attend Brown University. She was a gem of a woman, but I had no idea how to treat a gem at the time. My one and only goal was to get to her panties as soon as I could before any other brother on campus did.

One day while we were chilling in my room, I couldn't help myself as I extended my lips to kiss Brenda. "What are you doing?" she asked. "I'm trying to kiss you," I replied. "It's all good and everything, but just know that I'm a virgin and I don't plan on giving it up to anybody until I get married," she said with a serious tone. I'm a man and of course, I would try to push my limits. I figured Brenda never had sex because she never met a man that she was crazy about, and somehow my delusions of grandeur made me believe that I would be that man. We kissed and made out that day and it continued for the next couple of months. I remember that one time she rubbed on my dick so much, my balls were literally blue. I had enough. I wasn't gonna keep trying my luck at a brick wall anymore. Brenda had seen right through me. I finally gave up and I never got to taste Brenda's goods. There were just too may other women on campus willing to give it up for me to be waiting around on Brenda. She was a wonderful woman, but I had an impatient dick. I imagined getting lost in her pussy and that's exactly what it was, my imagination.

I had a lot of fun as a sophomore. Scotty and I still kicked it every now and then because he was still hooked on black girls. I had less of a hard time with my classes and I partied a little less. I also met a couple of professors who influenced me and opened my mind to the possibilities of the world. I also discovered literature and English. I was never an English fan, but one of my English professors made the subject fun for me. I also took a creative writing class that helped me delve into my creative side. I learned a lot about myself that year. I ended the year with a 3.9 GPA, just shy of a perfect 4.0. I was on the Dean's list during both semesters. Overall, I had a good year at Brown and I loved the school.

Junior Year

My summer break came and went. I can't even recall what I did that summer other than work and have a little fun with Kelly. Junior year was the year that I had to decide on a major and political science just wasn't doing it for me anymore. I couldn't see myself as a lawyer. I had found and discovered my creative side. I wanted to tell stories. I wanted to learn how to write and entertain the world with my writing. I was a pretty good writer, according to my professors. I wrote short stories of hope that depicted the plight of poor folks in the inner city. I tried as much as I could to enlighten my professors as well as my fellow students about black life in America. Some of the white students were still shocked that black folks could excel at Brown-even decades after we had the likes of W.E.B Dubois who excelled at Harvard. They still didn't feel that we belonged at Brown. I used to enjoy standing in front of the class to read my short stories and allow my fellow students to analyze my work. The questions were always surprising and thought provoking at times. There were students at Brown who had never interacted with black people. The only depiction of black life they knew was what they saw on television. They were engrossed in my stories and I educated them about my life and my common urban folks.

I also met Maria during my junior year, a sexy Puerto Rican chica from Providence. She was hot, fine, sexy and smart. Maria had never dated anybody out of her culture prior to meeting me, but we somehow managed to become pretty good friends and before I knew it, we were smashing regularly. Maria was an Eva Longoria clone with a Shakira body. We met in one of my English classes. She was having a hard time with an assignment and I offered my help. That first semester, we kicked it hard. We were always together and most people thought I was fucking her from the very beginning. However, Maria was not that type of woman. She made me wait half the semester before I even got a whiff of her pussy.

We were working on this project late one night, and I started to notice a different look from her. It was as if she suddenly found me attractive. Her dark piercing eyes and beautiful smile caught me by surprise as she sat there staring at me while I explained a complicated personification rule to her. I can't recall exactly what it was, but she was intrigued and started taking me in. I caught her just in time and I went for a wet kiss. Since I lived off campus in a one-bedroom apartment during my junior year at school, Maria and I were alone that night. I was anxious as my lips met hers and she unexpectedly stuck her tongue in my mouth. I enjoyed her kiss, but even more important I was drowning in her beauty. Maria had flawless skin, a petite waist, nice breasts and the perfect booty. She wore no makeup and she smelled sweet every time I saw her. I couldn't believe that I was finally kissing her. The physical awkwardness coming from us when we first started kissing soon went away and before I knew it, I had my mouth buried between Maria's breasts. I was taking her sweet smell in while leisurely sucking on her breasts. "Ooh papi, you do that so well," she said as my tongue circled her nipple.

Maria took her shirt off and dropped it on the floor. Her bra soon followed and I was working my way down towards her heaven. I licked her slowly until I got to her soft curly pubic hair, set in a heart shape around her pussy. I struggled to pull her jeans off at first because they were tightly fitted. After finally getting them off, I started eating Maria's pussy like a piece of fruit, my favorite nectarine. She struggled to control herself as my tongue took over her bottom half. "I want you to fuck me, papi," she told me. Without any hesitation, I slid on my condom and I proceeded to fuck Maria. She pushed her ass towards me as I went deep inside her. I pushed even harder as I held on to Maria's ass and saw heaven nearing. I fucked her gently until she started screaming out, "Papi, you're making me cum. Fuck me, papi." I elevated her booty and gave her my all. "Take it all, baby," I said to her as I stroked her. "Here it is, papi," she announced as her body went into convulsions. I stroked her a few more times to get a long nut out of her. That night, we fell asleep in each other's arms. Maria and I ended up together the whole year. Unfortunately, it wouldn't last too long because of circumstances beyond my control.

While school was going well and I enjoyed my new major in English, trouble was inescapable. The urban stigma was attached to my black ass and that stigma would end my scholastic career at Brown, as I knew it. There was a big party on campus and of course, I told Rammell and Kevin about it. As usual, they showed up for the weekend ready to party. Rammell came down from Williams College on the bus and Kevin drove with a couple of his new friends from Boston. It was the spring semester in April and I had just one month left of school before my summer vacation. I was ready to get my party on and hang out with my friends for the weekend. Well, my weekend didn't go exactly as planned.

After getting dressed and drinking a couple of brews before heading to the party, I noticed two of Kevin's boys were carrying switchblades with them like they were going to some party in the hood. I asked them calmly to leave their weapons in the car because it wasn't going to be that kind of party. They agreed and left their knives in the car. We walked into the party and it was packed. People were jamming and dancing to the hottest Hip Hop, R& B and Reggae. There were women everywhere. Most of the partygoers didn't even attend Brown University. There were people from Providence, Springfield, Boston, Worcester and the surrounding towns. Everybody was getting along great until a fight broke out. This dude from Providence started a beef because he felt disrespected by a few of the Boston cats, my boys. A fight ensued after words were exchanged and two people ended up stabbed. Of course, Kevin's boys acted like they had left the knives in the car, but they really stuck them in their shoes. I was confident they weren't armed because everyone was searched at the door.

It must've been a street thing because the other crew from Providence was also able to sneak their knives into the party as well. I couldn't stand there and watch Kevin and his friends fight without getting involved. I didn't think about the consequences or the repercussions. I just knew that I had to have my friends' backs. Rammell and I were swinging at dudes we didn't even know because they were gunning for us. One guy went to stab me, but Kevin got to him first. By the time police responded to the melee, everybody had fled the scene, but I wasn't so lucky. A couple of people identified me as one of the brawlers and I was arrested by campus police. Of course, I needed to keep my mouth shut about what I saw, so I acted like I knew nothing. After refusing to cooperate, the cops took me to jail. By then, Kevin, Rammell and his boys had taken off to Boston. It was a good thing they did, because if they had stuck around, Kevin would probably be in jail for attempted murder. I had to call my uncle to come bail me out of jail the next day.

By Monday morning, the school decided to expedite a disciplinary hearing to hear my case. I knew from the time I walked in that room, after looking around and saw nothing but white faces at the hearing, I didn't stand a chance. I was allowed to go back to class but they told me a decision would be rendered within two days. I wasn't really worried about the decision because I was in good standing at the school and was also on the Dean's list; however, the victim's parents were making plans to sue the school and I became a victim of their politics. They decided to expel me even though I wasn't charged with the stabbing or even involved with the stabbing. I wanted to fight the expulsion, but the angry part of me wanted to say, "Fuck the white institution and white people," and I did just that. I packed all of my belongings and took my black ass back to Boston without any plans for the future.

After I left Brown University, I didn't really want anything to do with anybody from there, including Maria. I liked her, but I didn't want to go back to Providence because of the incident that took place. My face was splattered all over the school's newspaper and I felt like I added to the stereotypes of black men in America. I was done with that chapter in my life, but I missed Maria. I cut all ties with her so she could focus on graduating, having been a first generation college student.

Disappointment

I felt like I let everybody down. I knew my mother didn't expect me to be a knucklehead, but she knew I was kicked out of school for the first time when I showed up with all my belongings at home. I kept the incident from her until a decision was rendered. I had also asked my uncle not to say anything to her. I really didn't know what to say to my mom. She was doing all she could to make sure I had a good life and I messed it up. I wanted to tell her how sorry I was, but it wouldn't fix the situation. When I saw the tears falling from her eyes and the disappointment on her face, I knew that I had failed her. "I'm sorry, momma. I was stupid. There's nothing else I can say." I was a little teary eyed when I told her I was sorry. My mother had never seen me cry, so she knew it was something significant to me.

I also had to tell my uncle that I was expelled. I presented the situation to him in a totally different light as far as the seriousness of the case. I had him believe that I was not involved at all in the fight and that I was a victim of circumstance. Well my ass was circumstantially kicked out of school. I had to tell him the truth. My uncle couldn't believe it. The only thing he asked was, "What are you going to do with your life now, Junior?" The only answer I knew at the time was, "I don't know." I didn't know what I was going to do with my life, but what I knew was that I didn't want to become a nobody. I didn't want to sit around and mope all day about what happened at school. I needed to move full speed ahead and achieve the goal that I had set for myself.

Getting expelled from school was one thing. I also had to fight the charges in court after I was arrested for reckless behavior, disorderly conduct and whatever else the cops concocted to get me locked up. Thanks to my uncle's connections, I walked away with a "continuance without a finding," which meant I had to keep my ass out of trouble for a year in order for the charges to disappear. If I was caught doing anything, I would be taken straight to jail to serve a sentence. My black ass had planned to walk a straight line.

My mother didn't say much to me during the first few days when I came back. I could just read the disappointment on her face. She wanted so much more for her child and I achieved so little. I had never disappointed my mother in the past, when I explained the situation to her she was a little more understanding, still disappointed nonetheless. I needed to make her proud again. I wanted to show her that her money was not wasted. I might not have gotten an Ivy League education, but damn it I was gonna get one.

Dusting Myself off

I wasn't happy with myself and I wanted to do something about it. I knew that I couldn't stay at my mother's house without contributing to the household. I decided to take a job at the bank while attending school at night, part time. I was going to get my degree one way or another and Suffolk University in Boston afforded me that opportunity. I applied and was admitted without any problems. I was able to request a clean copy of my transcripts from Brown University because I used to crush this girl who had a work-study job at the registrar's office. I don't know how she did it, but she was able to send a clean copy of my transcript to Suffolk University, less the expulsion. It took an extra semester, but I eventually graduated from Suffolk University in Boston with a degree in English.

Rammell also managed to graduate from Williams College. He was actually an inspiration to me because he had accomplished that feat a semester before me. We were all living in Boston and proud of each other. Kevin had chosen a different path. We worried about him but that was the life he chose. We just hoped he wouldn't become a statistic. We didn't want him to end up either way, dead or in jail. Rammell decided against graduate school and took on a position at the Boston Company earning a decent salary.

I should've been very happy that I completed my goal of obtaining my college degree, but for some reason I was not in a celebratory mood. My mother had to beg me to attend the commencement ceremony. She wanted to see her son walk across the stage with my degree in hand. She was proud and wanted to have a huge party to celebrate my accomplishment. My uncle was also proud of me because I didn't allow that incident to keep me from achieving my goals. However, since he came from Harvard University, I didn't feel I measure up to his accomplishments. I got my degree and I was happy to do it to please my mom.

I was able to save quite a few pennies while living with my mother. I helped her out with the household bills, but she never took money from me for the mortgage even though I offered. My car insurance was my only other expense. I wanted to buy my own place and I was focused on that. It took about a year, but I was able to buy a two-bedroom condominium.

All Grown Up

Since I moved back to Boston, I hadn't been hanging out with my friends that much. I kind of wanted to stay away from them to keep out of trouble. Kevin invited us to a party at his sister's house. I contemplated my decision before accepting his invitation. I hadn't seen his sister in years and I wondered what she looked like. Besides, it was also an opportunity to hang with my boys again. We had not hung out in a long time. All was forgiven about the past and it was time to move forward.

My focus was more on hanging with my best friends than anything. I hadn't a clue how the party was going to be and had no expectations. However, I did try to look my best. My body had become my temple and I worked hard at the gym to make sure it was well taken care of. I also took every opportunity to show it off. I wore a nice, white, fitted shirt, tan slacks, brown suede shoes, and a brown belt to match. My Burberry cologne was inescapable. I felt great and confident.

I walked through Kevin's sister's house at the party and I was almost mesmerized by her beauty. She had grown fuller and developed curves where I never knew existed. She was wearing a nice mini-skirt that accentuated her curvaceous body and sexy legs. Her fitted top suggested that she was a gym fanatic because only an annual membership at Bally's could help keep her stomach that flat. A perfect size twelve at 5ft 9inches tall without heels, and an even sexier woman at 6ft 1inch tall with heels, Marsha was fine as fine can be. I had never been with a woman as tall and big as Marsha and I wondered, in my own head, if I could handle her in the sack. I was a young scrawny kid when she last saw me almost eight years ago when Kevin and I were graduating from middle school. However, after developing to my full 6ft 2inch frame, Marsha's face came right up to mine for a perfect fit.

She had met this rich dude while attending college and they fell in love almost instantly. I can still remember the super, overweight lover. She brought him around to the cook-out my mother had for my graduation celebration. He was a huge teddy bear and his family owned more Laundromats in the Boston area than they could manage. His name was Hubert and his family had decided to pass the business on to him after he graduated from college with a degree in business administration. Because of my uncle, I was used to luxury cars and other things that impressed most folks in the ghetto. However, Mr. Overweight Lover drove a Mercedes 500 SL convertible, a car he could hardly manage to exit at times because of his weight. At least the few times that I'd seen him with her, he struggled to get out of the car.

I was thinking to myself the first time I saw him, "How in the world does Marsha have sex with this big ass man?" The man was fat beyond belief and he talked like he was gasping for air. I would've said she was his meal ticket out of the ghetto, but she had just graduated from college herself with a degree in computer science and at the time, the tech world was paying beaucoup money. Marsha could barely get her hands around his fat gut to embrace him, but they looked like a loving couple.

"Hi Junior. How are you?" Marsha said when she noticed me gawking at her. I wasn't too embarrassed because Marsha flashed me a smile that I had never seen before and I could only conclude that my presence made her happy. "Hi Marsha. Long time no see," I said. "Wow!

You've grown up to be a very handsome young man. Maybe I should've waited another ten years before I got married," she said playfully. She may have been playing with me but Marsha's true feelings were written all over her face. "Would you like me to give you a tour of the house while we catch up?" she asked. "Sure," I responded.

Marsha and "Mr. Paper Stacker" lived in one of those exclusive neighborhoods in Newton, Massachusetts where black folks used to work as servants back in the day. Bingham Lane was a street lined with trees with huge Victorian homes and driveways that housed 2-3 BMW's or Mercedes at a time. Anybody walking through could smell the amount of money on that street. Marsha's house was the size of a mansion. As people stood around in the family room and the foyer snacking on hors d'oeuvre from the servers, I followed Marsha to the kitchen. "Where's your husband?" I asked. I could tell that my question was not welcomed by the expression on Marsha's face. "He had to run out because one of the machines broke down at one of the Laundromats. This man never takes a day off from work," she said, sounding a little frustrated. "Sorry to hear that, but you gotta understand that you can't have this lifestyle without a lot of hard work," I tried to comfort her. "Enough about my husband, what have you been up to? Are you still in school driving the girls crazy? Planning to get a big job after graduation?" she asked excitedly with curiosity. "I guess you don't know, huh?" "Don't know what?" she asked. "I figured your brother would've told you since he was part of the reason I got kicked out of Brown University, but I managed to get my degree from Suffolk," I said to her. "What! I didn't know you got kicked out of Brown. What happened?" she asked. "It's too long to go into, but I'm currently working at my uncle's brokerage firm because of your crazy ass brother, but that's my boy, though," I said to her. "I know you don't want to talk about it now, but I wanna know what happened and I will help you any way that I can, especially if my brother was the cause of it. I'm happy you were still able to get your degree," she said with a smile.

"How about you finish showing me the house?" I suggested. "Oh yes, the house. Well this is the kitchen. I had it remodeled after we bought the house, but everything else is left in its original form," she said. People in New England take pride in their Victorian homes and Marsha was no different. The house was a huge six-bedroom four-bath home with enough room to house three families. The sit-in kitchen was beautiful and very spacious. It was decorated with oak cabinets around the back wall, a center island with a stainless steel faucet, marble countertops and a matching floor. I had never seen anything like this home. From the kitchen, we made our way to the formal dining room where I saw a breathtaking china cabinet set against the wall and an antiquated dining room set reminiscent of the early twenties. From there we went to the formal living room that gave the house a feel of old Victorian royalty with a white chaise, couch, sofa, an oak wood coffee table and a Persian rug. Everything was breathtaking. As we made our way towards the second floor, I heard Marsha say, "You just grew up to be as fine as you wanna be, didn't you?" before tapping me on my behind. I had been working out at the gym at school, gaining about twenty pounds of muscle since my freshman year, and I had also developed a swagger that many women found irresistible thanks to Kelly. I chuckled at Marsha's comment because I knew I couldn't go there with her. The last thing I wanted was for Kevin to catch us in a compromising position, or even worse, her husband. I knew it wouldn't be long before Kevin came looking for me. This dude was probably the greediest dude that I knew, but there wasn't enough food downstairs to keep him there for too long.

Marsha walked me through every room, including the rooms for her future children, guest room, her powder room, bathrooms, husband's office and finally her bedroom. "So this is where the magic happens, huh?" I said to her as we stood in her humongous master bedroom. "What magic? I wish," she revealed surprisingly with disappointment in her voice. "I'm sorry," I quickly apologized. "No need to be sorry, my husband was never a great lover to begin with, but I thought I could live with it," she said sadly. I didn't understand how she could marry a man that didn't satisfy her sexually. According to surveys, fifty percent of marriages end up in divorce because of lack of sexual satisfaction from a partner. I guess she figured his wallet was gonna make up for her sexual deprivation. "Why don't we just go back downstairs to join the party," I suggested. "I want you to hug me,' Marsha said out of the blue. Her request was a little awkward considering I was standing in the middle of the bedroom she shared with her husband for the last five years or so. Also, I didn't want him to walk in to find me hugging his wife. Sure, he knew me when I was a young kid, but I had grown up to be a man with a hard dick for his fine ass wife. "I really need a hug," Marsha begged. I was apprehensive at first, but I wanted her to feel good. I wrapped my hands around her body tightly to make her feel like she was deserving of compassion. It was as if Marsha had never hugged a man my size the way she wrapped her hands around my fit body and didn't let go for about 60 seconds. Her sweet smelling perfume was irresistible, I wasn't sure if I wanted to let go either.

As we hugged, the sweet scent of her perfume invaded my nostrils and I could not help developing a boner for this fine woman who so needed my affection at that moment. She could feel my bulge against my stomach. My face became flushed with embarrassment. "I'm sorry. I didn't mean to..." Before I could finish my sentence, she raised her hand to my lips and said, "I needed that. For a long time, I didn't think I could turn another man on." Was I hearing her correctly? I know that fat bastard didn't make her feel inferior, was what I thought to myself. "You are fine and beautiful. Any man in his right mind would want to get with you," I told her. "Well, my husband doesn't seem to feel that way. He only uses the hole between my legs for 30 seconds once or twice a month to get his shit off without giving a damn about me. I don't know if I can go on like this," she revealed. I really didn't know what to think, but I pulled Marsha towards me and before I knew it my tongue was in her mouth wrestling sensually with hers until I heard Kevin's voice coming from the stairway screaming my name. I was lucky Kevin's loud ass announced himself; otherwise, I would have been caught with my tongue tied in his sister's mouth.

"What y'all doing up here?" he said. Marsha quickly took over because I had no idea how I was going to respond to Kevin. "I was giving Junior a tour of the house," she answered. "Shit, that can take all day in this big ass house. Y'all have fun while I go downstairs and flirt with some of your fine ass neighbors," Kevin said before rushing back downstairs. I kept my hands in my pocket the entire time to keep my bulge from his sight. I was relieved that I didn't get caught, but I couldn't help pushing Marsha towards the door after closing it. I then stuck my tongue back in her mouth as my hand reached between her crotch to find her welcoming wet pussy awaiting my finger's arrival. My mouth went straight from her northern lips down to her southern lips as I stuck my tongue inside of her, eating her as she stood against the door with her legs wide open and her skirt up to her waist.

I don't know what came over me but I wanted to make Marsha feel good even if it was just for a moment. The heavy breathing started as she reached down to my fro and stuck her finger in my well-maintained Lenny Kravitz hairstyle. I had decided to grow my hair after I graduated from college. It gave me a distinctive look and the ladies just loved running their fingers through it. "Oh shit, it feels so good. I haven't had my pussy licked in over two years," she hissed. Marsha's sexual deprivation was coming to light by the minute. I inserted my index finger from my right hand in her pussy while my tongue rested on her clit, wiggling lightly. My right hand found comfort on her round booty as I continued eating her as if she lived alone and she didn't have a house full of guests downstairs. Nothing else mattered at that moment except her sexual gratification. I wanted to make her cum at all cost. As my hand continued to palm her ass, my tongue hungered for more as it wrestled with her clit, massaging it softly and delicately. "That's it baby," she murmured softly as my tongue went up and down her clit vertically. I repeated the same motion over and over until Marsha's legs started caving under her. "I'm cumming. You're making me cum, Junior," she said with tears in her eyes. It was as if this woman had not reached an orgasm in years.

After allowing her a complete recovery from my tongue treat, I stood up and gave her a kiss before walking back downstairs to join the party. I don't know what prompted me to do what I did, but I knew that Marsha felt a lot better, as did I, and it was also the beginning of a relationship that would change my life forever. I went back downstairs to find Kevin harassing one of his sister's pretty friends. Kevin wasn't one of the best looking guys that I had ever seen, but he had that bad boy swagger that many women like and this chick was playing a cat and mouse game with him that she had no business playing. Her husband was in the theatre room watching a football game with the rest of Marsha's husband's friends, not paying her any attention at all. As I made my way around the party tasting all the different hors d'oeuvres, I noticed how desperate and horny some of these rich women were. A couple of women vying for attention even surrounded Rammell.

My mind was now on none other than Marsha. I wanted her and I wanted her badly. Marsha was going to get it from me, and she was gonna get it real soon. We made eye contact a couple of times inconspicuously without allowing the party guests the opportunity to figure us out. I could still taste her nectar in my mouth and my dick was screaming for a voyage through her sugar walls. Marsha's walk was sexy and inviting as she made her way around making sure that her guests were comfortable. I didn't see too many of the hoodrats that she had grown up with when we were young. Her friends were a lot more sophisticated now and they all seemed to live lavish lifestyles. I knew that most of her guests were prominent because of the slew of German engineered cars that crowded her long driveway and the area surrounding her house. It was a ritzy party with all the thrills and frills needed to make rich people feel good about themselves. I had been to a couple of those parties at the homes of a few of my classmates when I was at Brown University. These rich people seemed to have had an endless supply of food and alcohol. Back in the hood, when I went to parties, the food and drinks usually lasted until about one o'clock in the morning, if we were lucky.

Flirting Around

It was almost midnight and Marsha's husband hadn't returned home yet. I could see she was frustrated and worried. Everything seemed to have been habitual, but it still bothered her. She was talking to her friends when she looked over her friend's shoulder and noticed me winking at her. A smile flashed across her beautiful wet looking lips and I felt a little tingle inside. Wow, I thought. She was really gorgeous and sexy. I was starting to feel confident that I might actually have a chance with Marsha. I wasn't gullible to think that she would leave her husband for me, but I was willing to be that source of comfort she needed in her life. It felt good knowing that Marsha had me on her mind. I smiled back at her and made sure she could read that "I wanna tear your ass up" look across my face. I didn't so much want to tear up Marsha as much as I wanted to make her feel wanted and needed. I wanted her to be a little happier even if it was just for the moment.

Neglect was written all over her face, and her facial expression revealed her sad stories, whenever she talked about her husband. As Marsha continued entertaining her guests, I motioned my head towards upstairs, while I stood in the background admiring her. I felt the need to finish what we started earlier. I wasn't trying to disrespect this man's house, but he wasn't doing what he needed to do to make sure his house was a home. Marsha ran her hand through her shoulder length hair as if to create a new way of communicating with me. I winked at her then walked away. I had no business walking up the stairs to the woman's house unaccompanied. I knew I needed to be patient because she had to play host for her guests. I also didn't want her husband to get back sooner than expected either.

I was in the kitchen standing by the fridge drinking a beer when I felt a sensual hand upon my right buttock, then a squeeze. All I could think about was Marsha trying to flirt with me in the midst of the crowded room due to all the excitement. However, to my most delusional disappointment, it was one of her neighbors, who had been eyeing me since I walked through the door. She wasn't my cup of tea, but I would do her on a slow night after a few drinks. I'm not trying to say she wasn't attractive, but I was not attracted to her at that moment because I was thinking about Marsha. I realized when I was in college that any woman could be attractive depending on the circumstances. One great example of that were the very few black women we had on campus at Brown. When I first arrived on campus, I didn't particularly notice anyone that stood out except for Crystal, but after being on campus for about three months around these hundred or so black women who attended the school, even the least attractive ones started to look attractive to me. However, when I took them out of the campus element and to the mainstream world, where other beautiful black women existed, they were very sub par aesthetically. With this particular woman who was groping me in the kitchen for no reason, that was the case. I could see the possibility of beauty in her even though it wasn't present at the time.

"How ya doing, handsome?" she said almost in a drunken stupor. Her breath reeked of alcohol and her advances were unwelcome. I stood there watching this woman trying to make a fool of herself and wondered where her husband could be, because she was wearing a three carat diamond wedding ring and band that almost blinded me. Are the women on Bingham Lane really that desperate? I thought to myself. Trying to be polite, I answered, "I'm fine," without leaving room for more conversation. "Lonnie, are you being bad again?" asked another woman walking by. Lonnie just smiled then reached for my pecks. "You work out, I see," she said as she ran her hands across my chest to feel my hard pecks. I was embarrassed a little, as she started to draw a little too much attention on herself and me. With beer in hand and a gaze to nowhere, I quickly made my way out of the kitchen, leaving the woman standing there foolishly. I didn't want to entertain her action and I felt it was best if I walked away.

One Thing Led To Another

Upon taking my first step into the living room, Marsha grabbed my hand and said, "I don't think I showed you the study and my collection of books. We took a few steps towards a wide hallway before she led me into what looked like a small library. The walls were lined with shelves and books. A nice wooden desk sat in the center of the room towards the wall, and a high back leather chair sat behind the desk. Not sure if she had locked the door behind us, the temptation to take her on the table was interfered with fear of her husband busting through the door to pull me off her, so I chilled. I walked around the room slowly without saying much for about thirty seconds before she said, "Don't worry, the door is locked and nobody should be coming this way." I knew it was her way of saying let's get on with the fucking already. It was as if my dick was hit with a thousand dose of Viagra. It shot up so quickly. "Wow, you're happy to see me, huh?" she said teasingly. I couldn't do anything but smile. "Come here and let me see why you're so happy," she said. Marsha sat me on the edge of the table as she pulled out my hard dick and took it in her mouth. "One good turn deserves another," she said. I was thinking to myself, you're right.

The warm tunnel in her mouth was soothing, as her lips took shape around my dick. Like a snake climbing up a tree, Marsha's tongue was spectacular as it went up and down from the shaft of my dick down to my balls. Afraid to be heard accidentally by a guest, I held in my feeling of excitement and contained myself while enjoying the blowjob of a lifetime from Marsha. "Nice, thick and long, I haven't tasted one of those in a while," she said between licks. I stood there like a super hero with my hands on my waist and beating my chest knowing that Marsha appreciated my dick. She used her tongue to do something that had never been done before and I almost collapsed on the desk. As I stood there watching her and pulling her hair, Marsha brought her tongue to the base of my dick, near my nuts and twirled her tongue hard enough for me to pull away because I didn't want to come that quickly. I was thinking that her husband must be a complete idiot to leave this woman sexually deprived.

Like a cheetah looking up at a prey, Marsha started making her way back up towards me with her eyes fixated on unfastening my belt and a look on her face that made me want to stick my dick deep inside her. By the time we locked lips, I had her skirt above her thighs, my pants and boxers down by my ankles and my dick ready for penetration. I turned her around to face the door as I stood with my butt still leaning on the desk. I leaned her forward, pulled her thong to the side and I penetrated her raw without even realizing it. My strokes were nice and slow as she took all of me in her. "You can't cum inside me," she said as my rhythmic strokes flirted with her sugar wall. I knew she didn't want me to stop because she kept pushing her ass against my dick to receive my deep strokes. She moaned softly and almost begged with her body language for me to fuck her harder. I could tell that Marsha was a freak- waiting to unleash her freakability on the right man. I grabbed her ass cheeks and stroked her forcefully a few times. With the gyration of her thighs and ass cheeks against my dick, I knew she would soon climax. I stood still, tight and hard to allow her to get her nut off. I stroked her a couple of times before pulling my dick out to let her take my protein down her throat. I could see relief on her face because she allowed me to see that it had been a long time since she had an orgasm that way.

Satisfied with our tryst, Marsha and I fixed our clothes before heading back to join the party. No words were exchanged between us, but Stevie Wonder could read the look of satisfaction on both of our faces. I knew then that I was going to be Marsha's regular fix. There was no way she was gonna have sex with me just once and never see me again, I thought confidently. The whole thing was exciting to me and I was looking forward to more. Unfortunately, fifteen minutes after we left the study Marsha's husband walked in. Our little flirting episode was over and I had to be on my best behavior for the rest of the night. I didn't want us to be found out by her husband, but more importantly by her knucklehead brother, Kevin.

Having A Good Day

I still couldn't believe that I had just had sex with one of my best friend's older sister, and the pussy was real good. I was no fool to think that any kind of romance was going to be flourished between Marsha and I. However, I did hope to visit her southern terrain a few more times. Marsha's taste was still on my tongue after I joined the rest of the fellas in the theatre room to watch the football game with Hubert and the rest of his white collar neighbors. Rammell, Kevin and I were clearly impressed with all the men who were present at the party because of their accomplishments, but none of the men seemed to be dedicated husbands who put their wives' physical and sexual needs at the forefront of their schedule. "These ladies should feel lucky that they are able to stay home and live a lifestyle that most women would die for," said one brother who was a stockbroker. Ranting about their high six-figure and even seven-figure salaries was the norm in between commercial breaks from the game. After introducing ourselves to the group of almost twenty men, whose names we could care less to remember, we had officially earned the nickname, Young Buck. They kept referring to each of us as Young Buck.

These guys felt the need to school us about women and the better things in life. We would've welcomed their lesson if there wasn't too much flair of arrogance attached to it. These "know-it-alls" felt their money gave them access to everything in the world, including indiscretions with young beautiful women. "Look, you can't disrespect your home. You can't give your concubine access to your wife," said the cool white boy named Jake who felt his

wife's ten additional pounds after giving birth to three
children was too much for him to bear in the bedroom.
"My wife gets it once or twice a month and that's enough
to keep her satisfied. She's lucky I'm even able to get an
erection with her fat ass," he continued. I had seen his wife
earlier and she was no bigger than a size 8. These white
boys must really love skinny women, I thought to myself. I
wondered how the few brothers in the room must've felt
hearing this white boy call his size 8 wife, fat, when their
wives were more on the 10-12 side of the fence. To my
surprise, the brothers agreed because their side dishes
were all sizes 6 or smaller. Those long hours at the office
at night weren't always spent working, according to these
men.

"No man can be with one woman for his entire
life," said one brother as everyone hi-fived each other in
agreement. Rammell, Kevin and I felt these guys were
leading double lives except for Hubert who said nothing
and never agreed or disagreed with anything that was said.
It was clearly understood why he wouldn't agree or
disagree in the presence of his young and impressionable
brother-in-law, Kevin. I couldn't fathom Hubert having
more than one woman. I couldn't even grasp my mind
around the fact that Marsha even had sex with him.

After watching the game with these buffoons, I felt less
guilty about having sex with Marsha. Something in my gut
told me that her husband didn't go out to make sure a
machine was being fixed. That little "Boys Club" revealed
enough about themselves for me to form my own opinion
of every single one of them, except for Harry. He was the
outsider who said absolutely nothing while he was in the
company of these men. It appeared as if Harry decided to
watch the game with these guys because he didn't want to

be a party pooper. Clearly, Harry didn't agree with the opinions and the shenanigans of these men, because he felt very uncomfortable in their presence. A balding father of two who feels lucky to have a beautiful family, Harry appeared to be the only faithful husband.

As much as these men bragged, I couldn't find any reason why any woman would throw herself at any of them, except for the fact that they had money. Bulging guts were common among them. Boring style was the norm and they were corny at best. Women have a knack to detect charm from certain men, and perhaps that's what may have happened with their wives. Their money may have also played a factor. I couldn't see it happening for them any other way. Overall, my friends and I had fun at the party and those clown ass husbands were the butts of our jokes on the way home. Still, I wondered, if they weren't satisfying the needs of their wives, who was?

The Rendezvous

I kept feeling the mounting pressure from my uncle to be something that I wasn't cut out to be-a broker. I hated that job with a passion and I wanted to quit as soon as I found something else that could earn me a good living. I managed to buy a two-bedroom condo in Hyde Park, Massachusetts with my hard earned salary when I was working at the bank. However, after I was laid off, my condo almost went into foreclosure. I had no choice but to take that job with my uncle. I had to hustle everyday to earn my paycheck, as the economy was sloping downward, courtesy of President Bush. The cold calls got on my nerves. The rejections from potential clients left me disappointed, most of the time, but I needed the gig and I was grateful that my uncle was able to help me get my Series-7 license and my brokerage license so I could have a job. I began to invest my money in real estate as the market started going bust. I got more deals than I could afford, but I managed to buy a few multiple dwellings at a discounted rate in foreclosure. I was trying to set my path to independence. I hated my job with a passion.

I received a text about eleven o'clock in the morning from Marsha asking how my day was going. I told her it was going well and then she followed with another text asking if I was available to talk. Since my uncle owned the brokerage firm and everyone knew that I was family, I had to work twice as hard. I didn't want any of the other brokers to think that my job was handed to me, so I made sure I stayed busy at work and kept a list of high profile clients that supported my paychecks and lifestyle. Since I hadn't gone to lunch for the day, I decided I would take my lunch at one o'clock so I could call Marsha.

"Hey, what you doing for lunch?" she said in another text, five minutes later. "I was hoping to grab a quick bite then come back to work," I told her. "Want some company?" she asked. "Sure. What would you like to eat?" I asked through a text. "It doesn't really matter. I just want to be in your presence. I wanna see you," she text back. Since I worked downtown and she lived all the way out in Newton, I needed to make sure she had enough time to come downtown to meet me. "I would like to see you as well," I responded using my Blackberry. My fingers had become very nimble and quick since I got my Blackberry. It also allowed me the luxury of multi-tasking.

I was on the phone with a client while carrying on a conversation with Marsha via text. The thought of seeing her again brought me back to the party at her house and I almost developed a bulge in my pants. Five minutes later, I received another text from Marsha asking if I wanted to forgo lunch and meet her at the Park Plaza hotel on Boylston Street near downtown Boston. My dick took over immediately. Who needed food? I didn't. I had a big ass bowl of cereal and a banana before I left my house that morning. I was good. Pussy is always better than food. One o'clock couldn't come fast enough. Shit, I was the most productive those two hours leading to one o'clock than I had been all month. I must've closed four or five deals in the span of two hours.

Not only is the Park Plaza a 5-star hotel, I had 5-star pussy waiting for me. I lied to my uncle and told him that I needed to go to the Registry of Motor Vehicles to fix something with my license. He knew all too well how long any trip to the RMV would last. I bought myself at least an additional hour with Marsha with that lie. It was not habitual for me to take long lunches at work, and the fact that I closed a few deals before I left bought me a free pass from my uncle.

It just so happened that I was wearing one of my favorite Ralph Lauren three-button, two-piece, navy blue suit with a light blue striped shirt, light blue silk tie, black belt and black shoes. My neck and wrist reeked of Armani Code by Giorgio Armani. I caught a cab from Washington Street down to Boylston Street and I got there just ten minutes after one o'clock.

I received a text with the room number from Marsha before I reached the hotel. I went up to the seventh floor and knocked on the door as she expected. I was surprised to find a sexy amazon of a woman standing in 5-inch heels, wearing a lace teddy, flawless make-up, and a hungry look in her eyes. She looked just as hungry as I did and I aimed to fill her appetite as well as mine. She also ordered lobster, vegetables, mashed potatoes and a bottle of wine for lunch. While she cared about feeding the hunger in my stomach, I wanted to feed her need for an orgasm. Lunch would have to wait as I reached for Marsha's glossy lips the second after I closed the door behind me. The strawberry colored lipstick smudged all over my lips as I took Marsha's full bottom lip in my mouth, savoring her minty breath while I kissed her passionately. My hands quickly wandered down her round ass while my hard erection rubbed against her crotch. I brought my hands up to hug her while we continued kissing and allowed her hands to grip my butt. She squeezed and I gave her more tongue. I took her tongue in my mouth, sucking it lightly enjoying whatever taste was in her mouth. Her voluptuously toned body was calling my name and my mouth was soon attached to her right breast.

I sucked her succulent nipple until the sensation forced her to whisper in my ear, "I want you to fuck me." No sooner did she say that, my jacket dropped to the floor.

My pants and boxers barely got passed my thighs before she reached out for my nine and a half inches of pleasure, rolled a magnum condom down on it, and stuck it inside her while we stood against the wall. It would take too long to make it to the bed and our patience was wearing thin from the time we laid eyes on each other. With her panties pulled to the side, I penetrated Marsha's wet pussy and began to stroke her. I held one of her legs up on my forearm as I allowed all nine and a half inches of my dick inside her. I could feel her wall on the tip of my dick as she moaned for me to fuck her. "Fuck me, Junior," she whispered loudly. It was a loud whisper only for my ears. I proceeded to wind and grind, catching a rhythm that was too good for both of us. I brought her leg down allowing her inner thighs to clamp down on my dick while I stroked her. Her pussy was dripping wet and my dick was hard as steel as I gave her my longest strokes. "I wanna cum, Junior. Make me cum," she begged. I grabbed her ass cheeks as I pound her pussy to an orgasm. My rapid short strokes were just what the doctor ordered as Marsha's body gave in to me. "I'm cumming, Junior!" she screamed. "I wanna cum with you I said before sticking my tongue in her mouth. The intensity of the kiss added to the sensation of my nut as I let out a good half an ounce of protein in the condom inside her. Her juices flowed down her thighs before she collapsed to the floor. Sweaty, with my pants and underwear still around my ankles, I helped Marsha to the bed.

Opportunity Comes Knocking

Marsha and I were exhausted, so we took a few minutes to recuperate before sitting down to have lunch together. During lunch, Marsha and I tried as much as we could to catch up on what had been happening in our lives. I told her how I loathed my job and that I would give anything to move on to something else, because I felt bad watching people lose their life savings all because of some bogus tip about a stock that I could make up to convince them to buy. People with money are gullible, as well as arrogant, because they have money, sometimes. However, when a guy called to tell me that he lost his kids' college fund because of me, I didn't feel good about it. "Have you ever thought about something else that you'd like to do?" she asked. As much as I wanted to leave my job, I never thought about what I wanted to do if I left. "No I'm not sure what I wanna do yet," I told her. "I know what you can do, and you'd be good at it, too," she said coyly. I was trying to figure out what she knew about me that I didn't know myself, but I came up with nothing. So finally I asked, "What do you suggest I'm good at?" I asked her. "Well, I don't want you to get the wrong idea about me, and I definitely don't want to gas you up" she said in a shy tone. "Go ahead. I'm not gonna get the wrong idea, and I'm not gonna be gassed up because I just ate," I assured her, humorously. "Well, since you're so good looking and good in bed, have you ever considered becoming an escort?" she asked nonchalantly. "What!" I screamed at her, with a surprised reaction. "I knew you'd get the wrong idea," she said disappointingly. "No, I don't have the wrong idea; it's just that my mind would have never gone there. How does one become an escort, anyway?" I asked her with curiosity. I saw a timid smile from Marsha for the first time, and there was something very naughty about it.

I wasn't sure where our conversation was headed but I was open to any professional suggestion that Marsha may have had. "I know when you came to my party you thought that my friends and I had the best lives because of all the money our husbands make. Unfortunately, it's totally opposite. Our husbands are cheaters, liars and most of the time, neglectful. We have a book club that we started. It has become our therapy sessions. We talk about all the emotional and verbal abuse that we endure from our husbands and how they make us feel fat and unwanted most of the time.   Hubert, even as fat as he is, has a mistress who lives in Dorchester. He pays her rent every month and takes care of her son. He thinks that I'm stupid and I don't know what he's doing, but he's no saint. He's a great provider, but that's about it. It's the same with the rest of his friends. They all have their little boys' night out when they go out with their mistresses," tears welled up in Marsha's eyes as she told me all of this. I sat back and just listened without saying anything. I was thinking that those assholes they call their husbands were either deliberate with their actions, or they didn't really give a damn about their wives. There was an awkward moment of silence after Marsha poured her heart out to me.

With my arms wrapped around her for comfort and my lips locked against her face, I asked, "What's all that have to do with me being an escort?" Marsha got up from the bed and walked towards the window before continuing with the conversation, "I know you won't believe me, but I have never cheated on my husband before. I enjoy the moments that I share with you, but I'm too connected to my husband to leave him. With that said, I want you to know that I'm not alone in the way I feel and I know plenty of women on Bingham Lane who would be more than happy to pay you thousands of dollars if you can make them feel half as special as you've made me feel when we are together." My eyes lit up and a light bulb went off in my head. "Are you serious?" I asked. "I'm dead serious. I don't really want to be emotionally wrapped into you, so the best way to keep from doing that is to share you with my friends who so desperately need to be treated special, even if it's once a month," she said. "How many friends are we talking about here?" I asked. "Almost all the women at my party; we are all sexually deprived and neglected, but we're too scared to leave our husbands because all of us are housewives," she revealed to me. I started doing the math in my head, estimating between $500.00- 1000.00 per woman and the figures were astronomical. "How would these women be able to pay for my services if they're housewives," I said, considering the idea. "Well, we all have monthly allowances from our husbands and we get to spend our money on anything we want. We'll be more than willing to sacrifice a purse, bracelet or shoes a month to get our self-esteem back," Marsha said. I got the feeling that Marsha was talking about herself, but she somehow managed to become the spokesperson for her friends.

The idea of being a male gigolo had never crossed my mind, but I was starting to think that maybe I could start this thing on a part-time basis before I acclimate myself to it while I was still at my job. I saw most of Marsha's friends at the party and they were pretty attractive to me, except for that one woman who was groping me. Sex was one of my favorite sports and if I could get paid for doing it without a camera in my face, why not? I thought. I never had aspirations of becoming a porn star, but I wouldn't mind being a closet freak. "How would you arrange all of this among your friends? And how are they gonna know that I can satisfy them?" I asked. "I'm sure you saw all the husbands at the party, and I can tell you that we all have the same complaint. Not one of those beer belly, ass scratching husbands is a stud in the bedroom. We married them because of the kind heart they had when we met them, not because of their sexual prowess. I'm sure they are all delusional enough to think that we are sexually satisfied by them, but that couldn't be farther from the truth. And when some of us do get it once or twice a month, which is rare, it usually last no more than five minutes." I couldn't believe that Marsha was giving me the run down like that on her life and her friends. Suddenly, I wasn't so envious of these guys anymore. "You have to understand that I have been trying to get my friends to take a bold step to satisfy their own needs and urges for a long time and then you came along. This is the best opportunity they're ever gonna have. You're sexy, you have a long, satisfying dick, you know what to do with it and you listen. That's what most of us need in addition to all the money that our husbands have," she said in a selfish way.

All that stuff Marsha said threw me for a loop, but I was definitely game to try it. Marsha and I talked about the plan and how she was going to present it to her friends and what I needed to do and how I was going to be paid. "I want you to know something, Junior. I like you, but I can't get all emotionally involved with you. And if you look at it this way, I'll get what I want and you'll have a new job that I think you may like better than the current one that you have," she said with a smile. Before departing, I needed to solidify my sexual prowess with

Marsha. My dick was like a steam pipe ready to burst as I pulled Marsha's underwear down to her ankles and stuck my hard, condom wrapped dick inside her from behind while she stared out the window overlooking Boylston Street. My hands found their way to her breasts and up and down her stomach while I stroked her from behind. "I want to fuck the hell outta your pussy!' I whispered to her. She could feel the voracity leaving my body as each stroke hit its mark up her vagina wall against her g-spot. "Give it to me, Junior! Fuck Me!" she begged. I did exactly that. I fucked Marsha for about fifteen minutes before she came all over herself again. I knew that I had to hurry back to work. I told Marsha we'd solidify the plans for me to start entertaining her friends later.

Lucky Fella

I had to contain my excitement on the way back to work. I couldn't believe that I was considering working as a woman-pleaser for a living. Most young boys grow up thinking that they could live the life of a porno star less the camera, but mine was actually becoming reality. I felt like a stud after leaving Marsha. I hopped and skipped back to the office like a little boy in toyland. The idea of sleeping with as many as twenty women alone was enough for me to think that heaven was on earth. As excited as I was, I couldn't tell anybody about my newfound hobby, job or whatever you wanna call it. Keeping my secret was gonna be key to my success, because I didn't want the ladies to get in trouble with their husbands. I also couldn't say anything to my friends because I didn't want Kevin to know that I was banging his sister. Rammell's mouth was bigger than a radio station, so shutting him out of my new plans was essential, as well.

Marsha called me back the following day. She provided me a break down of the husbands' patterns and schedules at work and at home. She also told me about this one particular woman who was the happiest out of all the women in her group, and once the women agreed to having me as their entertainer, this particular woman would have to be kicked out of the group, but those details would come later. Meanwhile, I insisted on Marsha not paying me to sleep with her. I was gonna be her personal master. Since she wasn't my mistress, I decided to become her master. She was gonna be the one to coordinate all activities between me and the ladies. It was almost as if she was taking on the role of a madam, but her only interest was the free dick she was getting from me. I told Marsha to buy herself something nice every week with the money she wanted to pay me with, and to consider it a gift from me. Marsha was the coolest chick I ever met. I always thought women were a lot more slick than men, but these women would confirm all of it for me as time went by. Marsha and I would have a couple more rendezvous before she brought the first woman to the hotel to meet me one day. It's not that the women didn't want to trust Marsha's judgment, but a second opinion was better than one.

The woman was blindfolded before I entered the room, and Marsha made it clear to her that she would spoil it for everybody if she took off the blindfolds. Marsha went downstairs to the bar, while she and I were left in the room alone. No pleasantries were exchanged as I walked up to her and started to kiss her softly. She was a white woman with a dark tan from one of those tanning salons. I could tell she used her salon membership daily because her tan was serious. She was probably a size 8 and weighed about one hundred and forty pounds. She ran her fingers across my chest to get a sense of my build. Satisfied with my tone, she pulled me closer and asked, "Are you gonna fuck me as well as Marsha said you can fuck?" "Fucking you well is my pleasure and my job," I said to her. My hands found her silicone hardened breasts and I was shocked. I had never felt fake breast before and her tits did nothing for me, but I had a job to do. So I proceeded to suck on her breast and from the reaction that I got, I could tell those breasts were only for show. All the nerves were gone as a result of her surgery. Her nipples barely got hard, but I sucked the hell out of those suckers.

I took her thin lips back in my mouth and attempted to French kiss her. Her tongue was soft and long. I sucked on it a little as her smeared lipstick got all over me. Her lipstick went above and beyond her lip line in an attempt to make her lips look fuller ala Angelina Jolie. As she lay on the bed on her back, I started making my way down her navel towards her wet pussy. It was dripping wet as my finger slid against her erected clit. "I want to feel your cock," she said. I obliged. I took her hand and placed it on my dick. "You have a huge cock," she said as she ran her hand up and down my dick. "I wanna give you head. I love sucking a big cock" she revealed. "Be my guest," I assured her. She sat up on the edge of the bed with her feet on the floor and I stood in front of her as she wrapped her long tongue around my dick. "Delicious. I just love sucking a big cock. It's been a while since I had one of those," she said between licks. She took my nuts in her mouth while she stroked my dick back and forth in her hand. I could tell that this woman enjoyed sucking my dick more than I was enjoying the blowjob from her, so I allowed her the enjoyment for a few minutes longer while I stood with my hands on my hips in front of her. The object was for me to please her, and not the other way around. "I can't wait to have your big cock inside me," she said. That was my cue to wrap my dick in a condom. I commenced the pussy attack.

I pulled her towards the edge of the bed with her leg spread wide like a gymnast, allowing her pinkness to obscure my vision. I couldn't just stick her. I wanted my tongue to connect with her pinkness. I knelt before her and took a whiff of her pussy before I made physical contact with my tongue. Her pussy smelled sweet enough. I was satisfied with her cleanliness, because you never know. Money doesn't necessarily equate clean pussy, so I brushed my tongue against the opening of her pussy while slightly tugging on her pussy lips. "Mm, that feels good," she confirmed. I went up a few inches to her clit that stuck out like a mini finger. I took it in my mouth and gently rubbed my tongue around it. "Oh shit! That feels so good. Don't stop!" she screamed. I continued to eat her pussy while my finger reached for her g-spot. "Oh shit! I'm coming," she said as she wind on my face and finger. She clamped her legs around my neck to allow herself the indulgence of a nostalgic nut that she seemed to have longed for a long while.

Content with my oral performance and the results from her, it was time to let her feel the wrath of my snake inside her. She braced herself for my penetration while at the same time welcoming my mandigo strokes inside her. "Oh yes, give me that big dick. Give it all to me," she urged. I didn't have too much of a handle on her ass, as much of it was nonexistent, I reached for her waist as I grinded slowly inside her with my dick reaching for her pelvis. "You feel so fucking good inside me. Fuck me!" she commanded. I pulled back a little to allow my perfect strokes to land on her g-spot. "You like this dick, huh?" I asked. "Yes! I love it. Give it to me!" she begged. I stroked her harder and harder like I was punishing her. The harder I fucked her, the more she begged. Then finally, I stuck my thumb in her ass as I increased the speed of my strokes. "Oh shit, I'm coming again," she announced. I couldn't leave the job half done. I pounced her pussy until she went into a trance. By the time I pulled my dick out of her to allow her to suck the semen out of me, she was drunk and shaking from the orgasm that she just experienced. The aftershock was evident as she continued to tremble on the bed long after I got dressed and was walking out the door. "That envelope on the dresser is yours. I hope that I can become a regular customer because you've earned every dime," she said.

That was the first time that I had ever been paid to have sex with a woman and I felt a little cheap, at first. However, upon opening the envelope to find fifteen crisp hundred dollar bills, my pride took a long vacation as I pondered how I was gonna live a lavish lifestyle fucking sexually deprived rich broads everyday. I never got that woman's name nor did I care. All I knew is that I put on a performance that would guarantee me future work. Marsha told me to make sure that she was satisfied and I delivered.

Marsha and I had established that none of the women would ever know what I looked like in order to protect my identity as well as theirs. The women would wear blindfolds during my encounter with them. The blindfold also allowed them a sense of anonymity because I couldn't make out their whole face. For all I knew, that woman could've had a glass eye or a crooked eye under the blindfold. However, since none of these characteristics were present at her party, I was somewhat confident that the rest of the woman's face was as pretty as what was revealed. The way that Marsha was able to ensure them that I was good looking, she brought a stack of pictures of fifty men to the women, including my picture, and she told them to comment on each one, and all the men met their approval physically with excellence. Marsha told me that they especially commented about how good-looking and sexy they found me. At the end, she simply revealed, "One of these men is going to please you, ladies, and that's all you need to know." She told me that's how she did it. The mystery of not knowing what I looked like made it even more exciting for the women. Each woman preferred to fantasize about the man she liked most in the picture and then envisioned that I was that man. The allure of the unknown got their panties more wet than I could have ever gotten them.

I later found out that the woman who slept with me was named Rebecca, Becky for short. Whether that was her real name or a pseudonym, I never cared to know, but she solidified my reputation as a good lover and the rest of the women couldn't wait to have their turn with me. Marsha called to let me know how Becky couldn't stop talking about me and how she would cum on herself every time she thought about the day that I fucked her. "I can concur with her because my pussy gets wet when I think about you as well," Marsha said. I was trying to walk a fine line because I didn't want Marsha to think that I was getting attached. She made her position clear with me and it was important that I maintained my distance, emotionally. I'd be lying if I said that Marsha was not special to me; there was something about her that could get a man caught up. Even with all the pussy that I had lined up waiting to be pleased, I still wanted to fuck Marsha more than anything. Perhaps it was the little crush that I had on her when I was a kid that resurfaced.

The "Ms. Jenkins" of the Suburbs

Sexing these women posed a certain kind of threat and danger to my life that I didn't think much about in the beginning. After sleeping with Becky, my clientele grew tremendously. I started having sex with as many as four women a week, making a total of six thousand dollars my first week with another group of women waiting and eager to get fucked. I was trying to figure out a way to rotate these women so everyone could be pleased at least twice a month, but it was almost impossible. Things were hard the first couple of weeks because I was still working my full-time job while trying to please these women. I was trying to do it during my lunch hour and my uncle threatened to fire me. It was also proving difficult on the women because they had to travel from Newton to Boston to come get their fix. The commute was forty-five minutes to an hour and it was wasted time, I thought. I finally decided to quit after enough of them made appointments to see me regularly. The best time to service these women was during the day because most of their husbands were at work and their children were at school.

Marsha and I set the rules and regulations forth and we were the only people who knew when I needed to go into a house because someone awaited my services. There were special signs that enabled me to know that it was an inviting situation. I also had a special signal for the ladies as well. With my signal, they knew that they had to open the door wearing their blindfolds while standing behind the door to allow me in, so the neighbors couldn't see them in their negligee blindfolded.

I decided to take on different professions and roles in order to frequent the neighborhood because there was a certain wannabe Ms. Jenkins who was the neighborhood's watchdog. The only difference was that she was white and she didn't live in the projects. Ms. Jenkins happened to be Cindy, the wife of Harry, the balding guy who never cheated on her. The ladies knew that she would never cheat on her husband based on the conversations they had during their book club meetings, so they decided to find a reason to kick her out after my services were confirmed. Cindy had been on a mission ever since to find out what the ladies were up to. There were days when I showed up as an insurance salesman, plumber, electrician and even as a Jehovah's witness, all courtesy of my research and friends whose cars I was able to borrow or switch for a day in my attempt to keep Cindy at bay. No one ever refused the offer to drive my convertible for a day.

Cindy was completely loyal to her husband and she found her friends to be knit picking and complaining all the time for no reason. It wasn't as if her husband was a stallion in the sack either, but she felt his money and the lifestyle he gave her more than made up for what he lacked in the bedroom. Often during these meetings, Cindy would be the one to coerce the rest of the group into discussing the actual book assigned for that particular week. These women met weekly and every week a new book was being discussed. They especially liked the erotic novels. I guess it was their way of killing two birds with one stone. Why not get complete satisfaction while reading a book? The mystery novels that Cindy often suggested were always overlooked and frowned upon whenever a steamier, sexier title was brought up by Marsha or any other member of the group. Marsha was a fan of erotica, and she was not interested in reading any book that wasn't going to get her pussy wet. Cindy almost seemed like a prude to them, but she was still their friends despite their differences.

My Homey Lover Friend

Marsha and I grew closer over time and there was nothing that she didn't share with me when she could. She kept me updated on everyone's household and who needed a good nut when they were stressed. We found ourselves laughing at what I was doing most of the time. After a while, it wasn't even about the sex between us anymore. There were times when I saw Marsha and all we did was talk. She was an interesting woman. I can always recall the story she told me about Hubert when they first met. They attended the same university and Hubert was this awkward guy that would sweat all the time. She would always see him around campus and he would greet her each time. However, one day he decided to go beyond the normal greeting and started talking to her. She knew he wanted to talk to her because he was soak and wet as he stood there gazing at her. "Are you ok?" she asked the sweaty Pillsbury doughboy look-alike when she saw him staring at her, sweating a river. At a loss for words, all he could do was shake his head "yes." She smiled at him then walked away. Everyday he met her at the same spot with a rose in his hand and little by little, he started opening up to her. She said Hubert was the most romantic man that she had ever met because he wrote her a poem everyday. What transpired after a two-year friendship was a romance forced out of pity. However, Hubert developed some self-esteem in the process, and he started opening up more. By the end of their first anniversary together, Hubert had become hugely popular, thanks to her. Everyone wondered how the fat boy was able to pull the fine girl.

While most people on campus thought they were an odd couple, Marsha started falling for Hubert more and more. When Biggie Smalls hit the scene, he was the role model that all big, not so attractive men, were looking for. Biggie's swagger was copied by most and the ones with money tried to dress like him as well. That was the case with Hubert. Marsha allowed him to be himself and Hubert discovered his other side. Though she left that part out, I knew one of the reasons that Marsha gave Hubert any play was because his family was paid. There weren't too many black college students riding around in a Range Rover on campus, but Hubert was. He was very kind with his family's money and Marsha benefited from his kindness. She didn't have to walk anywhere because Hubert had become her chauffeur whenever she needed to go somewhere. He took her to every concert, club, play and anything that was happening in Boston. They also went away on trips overseas together and he gave her the attention that every woman craved. Hubert was her big teddy bear. We were laying in the bed naked when she was telling me all this, so I needed to ask her one simple question, "How in the world can you sleep with that fat bastard? Sorry, I didn't mean to call your husband a fat bastard," I said apologetically immediately after my comment. To my surprise, she answered, "It was never about sex between Hubert and me. I grew to love and accept him for who he is. For your information, Hubert is pretty good with his tongue." I said to her, "He better be able to eat pussy, cause you'd need a jack to find his dick under that fat ass gut of his, that looks like a flat tire." She laughed at the joke, but I knew she didn't approve of it. I decided to stop being mean, because Hubert was her husband. In a way, I was trying to comfort her by making fun of him, but I could tell she had heard the crude jokes before, and it was time for me to stop.

We also shared other special moments together. I remember when Hubert forgot her birthday. She was sad about it the rest of the day. She never said anything to remind him about her birthday. I wanted to make it special for her, so I took her to Six Flags in Agawam, MA for the day. It was the summer time, so it was hot and Marsha decided to wear something a little revealing, so she could be comfortable. Marsha and I acted like two kids as we walked hand in hand. We rode every ride in that park. The park was a little less busy, because it was the middle of the week. We ate cotton candy, kissed while going through one of the scary rides, but most of all, she left her problems behind for the day because her husband's name never came up the entire day. I could tell that Marsha liked me a lot on that particular day. I knew that she knew I liked her too.

It was a long ride back to Boston and Marsha and I decided to do something a little exciting. I pulled over at one of the rest stops where I proceeded to eat her in the back seat of my truck. For some reason, Marsha knew to wear a skirt whenever she was going to spend time with me. It was rather sudden when I told her, "I'm gonna pull over so I can eat the hell outta you." "That sounds good. I hope you're hungry, cause I have a lot of food," she said playfully. Since my car windows were tinted, I felt safe enough to hop in the back seat and have some fun with Marsha. We were parked under a tree with the front of the car facing outward. The tree provided additional shade and darkness. It was about 5 o'clock in the middle of the afternoon and the sun was beaming. Marsha sat in the middle with her legs spread apart, while playing with her pussy. "Do you wanna get a little taste?" she teased with her finger after pulling it out of her pussy. Her shaven pussy looked good and the saliva in my mouth was running like a fountain. I was still in the front seat waiting to join Marsha who made her way to the back with ease. Driving a Chevy, Suburban had its benefits. "My pussy's calling your name, Daddy," she said while rubbing her clit. I reached for her finger and then put it in my mouth. Her nectar was sweet and my dick was about to hit the wheel. With my car on and the air conditioner blasting, I maneuvered my way to the back seat without getting out of the car. Marsha pulled off her underwear and rubbed it in my face. The aroma of her pussy had my dick hitting the roof of my car. I stuck my tongue out to her and she took it in her mouth. "I told you your pussy tastes good," I said to her. Now with our lips locked, one finger inside her wet pussy, we started making out.

As the passion started to heat up between us, I was getting ready to go down and start licking my favorite dish when we heard the sound of a baton beating against the window. I turned to find a State Trooper staring at us with this disgusting look in his eyes. I quickly fixed myself before rolling down the window to address the officer. I could see the embarrassment on Marsha's face as she quickly closed her legs to keep the officer from seeing her goods. "Sir, do you know that you can get arrested for what you are doing here," he said with authority in his voice. The last thing I needed was to be arrested with Marsha for some lewd behavior in public. I had to think of something quick. "I'm sorry officer, it's just that today is my wife's birthday, and after being together for so long, I was trying to bring some excitement to our marriage," I lied. I was lucky that there weren't any kids around. "Well sir, I'm gonna let you slide this time because I'm a married man myself, but we have people committing crimes around here and I have to do spot checks in the area. You all are gonna have to find another spot to spice up your relationship. Have a good day, sir." I guess we got lucky that the officer didn't arrest us. I said nothing back as I hopped behind the wheel and took off on my merry way with Marsha.

We laughed about the entire incident on the drive home, but we also thought about what the consequences could've been if we had gotten arrested. "Hubert probably would let me stay in jail and rot after hearing the charges," she said while laughing. "That shit ain't funny," I said to her while holding in my laugh. "I didn't even get to taste the pussy," I said sarcastically as if I was disappointed. "How about I taste you instead?" she said while moving the center console out of the way. My truck was high enough that no one could see Marsha sucking my dick while I drove. She unzipped my pants and before I knew it, her head was on my lap, while my dick filled her mouth. She was sucking away while I tried to stay focused on the road. Marsha was lying on her stomach across the front seat and I couldn't help reaching across her ass to stick my finger in her while she sucked my dick. I could feel her gyrating on my finger as I penetrated as much of it as I could from across the seat. Her pussy was hot and wet. I took the finger out of her pussy and into my mouth. She tasted so good and I wished that I could just spin her ass towards me and take her right on the front seat. Trying my best to keep from swerving on the road, I could feel a nut coming as Marsha wiggled her tongue around the shaft of my dick. I held on tight to the wheel while announcing to Marsha, "I'm coming." Like a mature woman, she swallowed everything with ease and even sucked a little more to make sure I got it all out.

We continued with our drive to Boston laughing and joking with each other. However, I felt the need to find out something from her. Unexpectedly, I asked, "How do you feel about the situation between me and your friends? Does it bother you that I sleep with these women for money?" Marsha turned to me and said, "Remember I'm the one who suggested it. You and I are cool, but I wouldn't get jealous over what you do. I've already told you that I'm not gonna leave my husband or family for any man. Your dick is good but it's not that good." She was trying to hold in her laugh, but I picked up the seriousness in her tone. I realized how committed Marsha was to her family, but she still needed sexual satisfaction. "You know Becky is still talking about how well you fucked her that day," she told me. "Really? I'm supposed to see her again in a couple of days," I revealed. "Be careful. It sounds like Becky might go crazy over some good dick. You don't want to be wrapped up in that drama. Try not to fuck too well," she said with a laugh. "I'll try my best to hold back some of this good stroke from her," I said jokingly.

Marsha's birthday ended up being special because she was special to me and I wanted to make sure she had a good time. Hubert didn't even bother calling her once to see how she was doing the entire time I was with her. I questioned her commitment to him. I wondered if Marsha was too scared to face the world on her own. In fact, I questioned if all the women on Bingham Lane were too scared to be independent. That was neither here nor there, because without their fear, I wouldn't have been presented this wonderful job as a gigolo.

Getting To The Good Part

Next in line for my services was this conservative, nerdy, and undercover hot thing named Sally. Her husband was a CFO at this mid-size company in Boston. He enjoyed fast cars, hoochie mamas, and partied like he was single. Making it home for dinner has never been part of his agenda. He made it clear to his wife that he had to work long hours and to compete with other employees in order to keep his lucrative job. His middle name should've been Flash. Everything about this man was flashy and he was as arrogant as they come. The square footage of his house was pertinent information in any type of conversation. He might as well have driven his Ferrari with the sticker price on it because he advertised it so much. His reasoning for marrying Sally was that she would never go out on him and she should be happy that she could be with a man like him. His money was his worth and everything else was shit. I got the breakdown about him from Marsha as usual. I figured out who he was at her party because he mentioned his cars so many times. I thought we were in an auto showroom with a salesman pitching to me.

Sally appeared to be a little nerdy when I first saw her. She was a typical Irish woman married to an arrogant Italian dude who thought he was God's gift to the earth. With her hair pinned up, wiry frame, a disappearing acting booty, and an almost nonexistent chest, I wondered what she was expecting from me. She was also on the thin side, no bigger than a size two. Sexy was definitely not the thought that came to mind when I saw her. I was looking at her and thinking to myself that I might break her in half.

She easily fit the profile of one those Hollywood superstars with an eating disorder. As much as she seemed to have been disappointing in size, I was in for a little adventure from Ms. Sally.

"How ya doing?" she asked nervously after I stepped inside her house. I didn't care much for small talk because I was there to do a job, but I appeased her. "I'm fine. Is everything cool with you?" I asked worriedly. "Everything is great. We have a couple of hours until I have to pick up the children, so why don't we get right down to business," she said affirmatively. "All righty then," I whispered under my breath. "Let's get down to it," I said. "I'm gonna need your help finding my way downstairs," she said, as reached her hand out to mine, so I could guide her. The blindfold was mandatory and there was no negotiating that. "There should be a door straight ahead that leads us downstairs," she told me. I took her hand, walked to the door, opened it and began our descent to the basement. I had never seen a sexual dungeon before, so when I got downstairs and saw what Sally and her husband had built, I was shocked. There was a Stockade with fully functional spreader bars, a set of five dungeon shackles, a chest rest and a devious fucking rod. There were chains suspending from the ceiling, a Liberator Stage Bed with straps on it, reminiscent of something that a person would find in a death chamber. There were also handcuffs, whips, dildos galore, vibrators, straitjackets, clit massagers, oils, dog collars, anal beads, gagging balls, whips and paddles, strap-ons and harnesses, sex swings and slings, and every other creepy sexual toy that one can imagine. "I'm sure you can already tell what I'm into from the décor in the room," she said. "Yeah," I said with a little reservation in my voice. "I hope I didn't scare you," she said timidly. Now all of a sudden this freak wanted to try to act timid and shit.

It was one thing to take inventory of the room, but it would be another thing to learn how to please this chick. I did what very few men with pride would, I asked, "What would you like me to do to you?" I tried my best to sound as sexy and appealing as possible. "I wanna be tied up and spanked before you fuck me in the ass. It's been a while since my husband spanked and fucked me in the ass. I also wanna be gagged while you're doing it," she revealed. That was some shocking shit for my ass, but I was game to try to get as freaky as she wanted me to be. Sally disrobed to reveal her skinny frame, and I was not impressed. "I don't mind sucking your dick before we get started, you know? I hear you have a huge cock," she said. I thought that maybe a blowjob might get the blood flowing because her naked body alone was not getting a rise out of me. Before taking off my clothes, I scoped the whole room for an escape route in case her husband made it home early. She must've been able to sense my hesitance, as she said, "You can go back to the top of the stairs and lock the door to feel more at ease. My husband knows that I come down here to please myself and I always keep the door locked because of the children. I saw one other door on the other side of the room. As I made my way towards it, she said, "That door leads to the backyard, but you don't have to worry about it because my husband ain't coming home anytime soon. Today is the day that he spends with his mistress. He doesn't think that I know about her, but I do. I was thinking that this shit was a common theme among these women. They all knew their husbands were cheating, but none of them was willing to do anything about it. After my blowjob, I knew I was gonna have to gag this chick because she talked too goddamn much.

I eased myself out of my clothes and made my way towards her. She did the normal thing that almost all of the other women did; she ran her hands up and down my chest and then around my face before she reached down for the cougar. "Whoa! Your cock is twice as big as my husband's!" she exclaimed. I wish you'd shut the fuck up and put it in your mouth already. How the fuck could she tell that my dick was twice the size of his when my shit was still soft? It didn't take long for her to wrap her lips around my dick engaging in a battle between big black dick and excited white girl's lips and tongue. The warmth of her mouth enabled the blood flow and my dick grew to its full potential in no time. Sally struggled to gain her composure as she excitedly took to licking the head of my dick like a happy puppy. "Your cock is a mouthful," she said after attempting to deep throat it. She started massaging my balls with her hand, as she went up and down my dick with her tongue. Her thin lips ran circles around the shaft, while she played with the head hoping to make me bust a nut. I can't say that it didn't feel good, "I want you to fuck my mouth," she demanded. I soon found my hand holding the back of her head as I humped her mouth. My dick was hitting the back of her throat hard and she was loving every minute of it.

I finally stopped fucking Sally's mouth before I took her to the Liberator Stage Bed that was set-up in the middle of the room. I strapped her to it. Her hands and feet were bound with her face against the bed and her backside facing me. "I want you to spank me well, "She said before I tied her to the bed and stuck that gagging ball in her mouth. I took the whip and started to spank her lightly with it. "I hope you don't fuck the way you spank," she said undermining my strength. This chick likes pain, I thought. "Here's your wimp," I said in my head. I reached my arm back as far as I could as I released the lasso of the whip against her pale skin. The sound alone made me quiver, but she surprised me when she said, "That's what I'm talking about." Oh shit! I might go to jail for fucking this chick up, I thought, because I was planning to beat the shit out of her like a master beat his slave. Before the thought could even form in my head, she yelled, "I want you to beat me like I was your slave." I began to take pleasure in beating this skinny white chick. "Take this!" I yelled as I swung the tail end of the whip against her flat ass. I could see the red marks forming on her skin, but she wanted more. By the time I was done beating this chick, I was exhausted. "Do you have enough left in you to fuck me in my ass with that big dick of yours?" she said sarcastically. I had to man up and fuck the hell out of this chick. I slipped on a condom so I could fuck her in the ass. With her legs spread against the bed, I took my hardened dick and started penetrating. All the while, I was wondering in my head if this white girl was gonna try to get my black ass arrested for rape or something. She had me doing some demonic shit to her.

"Fuck me and fuck me hard. I wanna laugh at my husband's little dick next time he tries fucking me in my ass," she said. I almost wanted to say, "Damn, do you even love your husband?" That was irrelevant because she was paying fifteen hundred dollars for me to humiliate her. She didn't even flinch as all my nine and a half inches went up her ass like Superman reaching for the sky. One hump, two humps, three humps and a long stroke…this chick was still talking about "fuck me hard." I wasn't working with much. Her ass was as flat as an ironing board, so the excitement only came from the fact that she wanted me to hurt her, something that I was not used to and didn't want to get used to. I swear, I barely had the tip of my dick in her ass as I brought my stroke up from down near my knees with force, up in her. I continued with the brutal strokes until she started screaming "Yes! I'm fucking coming! Yes. Fuck my ass!" I was glad that she came because my black ass was getting tired. I unstrapped her and she thanked me for a job well done. Little did she know she took every ounce of energy that I had. She handed me a sealed envelope with the only form of payment that I accepted, CASH. I really earned the fifteen hundred dollars she paid me. I made a note to myself that I wasn't going to do her weekly. She became a bi-weekly customer and the requests became more bizarre with each visit.

I felt comfortable doing five women a week, plus the extra sessions that I had with Marsha twice a week. Marsha paid for the posh hotels where we met for our rendezvous. It was business as usual and I got to live a lucrative lifestyle because of my bedroom skills, and I thanked God everyday that I'm well-endowed and blessed with the knowledge to please a woman. I was also lucky that Kelly lived below me. She was my first teacher and she'll forever be in my heart.

Kelly

I hadn't seen much of Kelly since I left my mother's house. We used to talk on the phone regularly, until she met this dude who wanted to have her on lockdown. Kelly was more than a teacher, a sex partner, and a booty call to me. She was a friend. We used to talk about my personal problems, as well as hers. She was actually the person who helped me through my ordeal after I was expelled from school. I felt like my world was coming to an end, because I disappointed my mother and my uncle. Kelly shone the light when I needed sunshine, and she made me smile when I was sad. She helped me come to grips with the fact that I had to lead my own life even though my mother and uncle had high expectations of me. She also helped me realize that I was just as much to blame for getting involved in that fight as Kevin did. She made me understand that if the roles were reversed, I probably would have done the same thing. There were a few little revelations in my life that I wasn't willing to accept yet and she made them acceptable.

Kelly and I were growing apart and I needed to come to accept that. Her children were also getting older and we couldn't do the things that we used to do back in the day anymore. I saw her for the first time in couple of years since I left my mom's house. It was a breezy summer day and I decided to visit my mother a little later than usual. My mom and I had a routine for visitation due to her work schedule. It was always best for me to visit her before 6 o'clock at night, but she was off on that particular day and offered to make me dinner. At 5:30 in the early evening, the sun was still beaming when I pulled up in front of my mother's house. I had just purchased my new convertible XK8 Jaguar. It was the hottest car on the road at the time. In fact, I was the only person who owned that car in Boston. I picked it up the day the manufacturer made it available in New Jersey. I had to be flown to Jersey to pick up the car. Rammel went with me to pick it up and we started getting numbers from the Jersey Turnpike all the way down I-95 to Boston. That car was hot and it was courtesy of this special lady that I met at a function.

I wore a fitted, white Gap t-shirt. It exposed the contours of my muscle tone. My loose fitting jeans and my brand new white on white air force ones made me look as crisp as a brand new dollar bill. She was headed towards me wearing a flowy linen dress. I knew it was her, because I was used to that walk since I was a little boy. Joy gripped my heart as I anticipated a big hug from her and perhaps even more, once we made our way inside her apartment. The closer she got, the wider my smile grew. Finally, she exposed her pearly whites as she laid eyes upon me. I almost felt like I needed some kind of theme music as I slow-motioned my way towards her for an emotional scene from a love story. I had been busy the last two years doing more than I cared to share with Kelly, but seeing her again did something to my heart. With my arms wide open, I reached for her embrace. She was a little more distant than usual. Perhaps it was because we were outside on the sidewalk where everybody could see us, I thought. "Hi baby," I said hoping she would pucker up and lay a kiss on me. Instead, I got a, "High Junior. You better hurry up and put me down before my boyfriend comes out here and makes a scene," she said. I had her up in the air in a bear hug. It was an unexpected surprise, but I eased her back down to the ground. "You never told me that your boyfriend was living with you," I said to her. "Junior, it's been two years since I've seen you. I figured you moved on and I did the same. Besides, you can't be tied down with an old woman like me," she said trying to comfort herself with the situation. When I heard the words "old woman," I was thinking that Kelly must be taking some bad crack because there wasn't anything old about her. She looked sexy as ever.

I was disappointed, but I had to respect her decision. There was no time for small talk, because her boyfriend was gawking at us through the window shade. "I guess that's it, Kelly," I said to her sadly. "Take care of yourself, Junior," she said before entering her apartment. I guess I was taking Kelly for granted and never realized it. I felt that she would always be around for me. She was the only special woman that I met, besides Crystal and Marsha. I always thought that I would end up with her. In a way, I was overly selfish as well. I visited my mother weekly and I never took the time to make my way downstairs to see Kelly, because I was preoccupied with a lifestyle that I wanted to live so badly. The amount of money that I was making as a gigolo was more important than me finding love. I purposely went to see my mother early because I knew that Kelly wouldn't be home. All the stuff that I thought was important, Kelly didn't even notice. She said nothing about my body, clothes or car. That's when I realized that I was becoming a vain asshole, whose purpose was to be a well-kept male ho. What the hell was I doing to myself? I questioned. Was I really happy with my life? Did these women justify my being? Was I wrong for sleeping with married women? I pondered these questions as I made my way upstairs to go have dinner with my mother.

I went upstairs and had a great time with my mom. We talked about what I was doing and of course, I lied to her. No mother wants to hear that her son is a male ho. She thought I was a real estate investor and my business was booming. I could see the pride in her face. I always treated my mother special. She received flowers from me twice a week and she didn't have to wait for mother's day, her birthday, or Christmas to get special gifts from me. I made it the norm.

Original Game

It had been a while since I hung out with my uncle. I was a little apprehensive about seeing him since I stopped working for his company, but I missed his wisdom and genius. I decided to give him a call and invite him to a Celtics game since he was a big fan. "Hey Junior," he said after picking up the phone on the second ring. "What's up, Unc? I replied. We talked for a while about the times we hadn't seen each other and he asked if everything was going well with me. I assured him that I was fine, and then we made plans to hook up.

In the past, my uncle would pick me up whenever we made plans to go anywhere because he was the big-baller driving a Mercedes Benz. He had traded his convertible Saab for the S class Benz. But this time, I decided to drive. I wanted my uncle to see how his nephew had come up. I pulled up in front of his house in my brand new Jaguar XK8 convertible, the first of its kind. I called him on my cell phone to let him know that I was outside. My uncle's jaw almost hit the floor when he saw my car. Since I was making beaucoup money, I decided to live it up a little. I got a deal on a factory rebate and I ended up paying almost $10,000.00 less than what the car was worth. I didn't even want to mention to him how I got that car. I knew that I had to stay a gigolo for a long time in order to keep it. And I especially had to keep fucking this fifty-five year-old widow whose pussy needed more than lubricant every time I fucked her. She was loaded and spending money on me like I was an armored truck company picking up deposits daily from a bank. Her billionaire husband died and left her everything. They had no children and she didn't seem to have any close relatives. I had to bring her ass to the theatre, opera and all the other classy shit that rich people do. She didn't mind showing off her arm candy to many of her friends, but I dreaded fucking her.

Anyway, the first thing out of my uncle's mouth was, "How in the world are you able to afford a car like this?" I wasn't quite sure if I should be honest with my uncle about my new line of work, so I lied. He already knew that I got into the real-estate game early and I sat on a few multi-family units. I lied to him and told him that I sold a couple of them and came out with a $400,000.00 profit and I bought myself a gift. It wasn't unreal to make that kind of profit from the sale of a house at the time. Most of my homes were bought for less than $100K, but when white folks drove the housing market to its peak, I was able to pull almost $350, 000.00 worth of equity out of the four homes that I owned. I was sitting on a pretty penny and I was earning even more money with the ladies.

"Damn, I'm jealous, Junior. I was waiting til my fiftieth birthday to get this car and here you go at fucking twenty four years old driving my dream car," my uncle said as he walked around the car, admiring every curve and line of the design. When I opened the door to let him in, it was a wrap. After he sat on the plush leather seat, making himself comfortable, I said to him, "Come on, Unc, you know you can afford to buy that car now. Your ass is just being cheap." "Not everybody can live as freely as you, Junior. Now let me tell you something; with a car like this, you're gonna get more pussy than you can afford to fuck. So you're gonna have to be careful with the women you meet out there. A car like this spells money and you're gonna get a lot of gold-diggers who are going to want you for your money," he told me as if I didn't already know. "I know, man, but I'm ready for them," I assured him. Little did my uncle know, I had no time for those gold-digging honeys. I was fucking more women than Hugh Heffner and I was getting paid to do it. I wasn't gonna waste my time chasing after pussy. However, on the ride to the game, my uncle felt the need to continue schooling me about women. This is the same dude who swore he wasn't going to get married and have children until he was about sixty something years old and walking around with a cane and a limp dick. "Junior, I hope you understand that just like men, women also have options. Don't be fooled by the fact that they outnumber us and that it doesn't give them options. As long as a woman has a pussy between her legs, she'll always have options," he went into a diatribe. I had no idea where the conversation was headed, but I allowed him his moment. He continued, "You see, unless you're ready to commit to a woman, you have to position yourself as the option you want to be in a woman's world. Most women have two or three men that they're eyeing or would like to be with for the rest of their lives, but often times, men have placed themselves as a top option when they're not even ready to commit to a woman. What I mean by that is, if you meet a woman and she feels that you have it going on; you have a good job, education, you're articulate, good looking and have a good head on your shoulders, you automatically become that woman's first option. The two other guys may just be filling space and time until she's ready to snatch your ass up." I'm sitting there listening to my uncle's attempt at making sense of women and their needs regarding relationships. I realized that he might be right with some of his points. I didn't interrupt. I continued to listen. "Junior, you're a young man and you're successful. You need to enjoy your life before deciding to settle down with that special woman. Oh yes, there's a special woman out there for you, and you'll know her when you meet her, but until then, you need to make yourself option number three on every woman's list," he said.

It's not like I was planning on settling down any time soon, but my uncle felt the need to school me on relationships and I appreciated it, somewhat. The way my life was going, I didn't foresee marriage in the near future at all. However, it made for good conversation, so I continued to listen. "Junior, the way that you make yourself the third option on a woman's list is by making yourself the least available to her. You can't be cuddling with a woman everyday, seeing her often, and not expect her to get attached to you and want to become one with you. That right there gotta stop, if you ain't ready for a relationship with that woman. You have to give her as limited access to you as possible if you want to remain option number three. You can't be sending her flowers regularly, taking her out to eat, taking long walks on the beach, staying on the phone all night long with her and expect her to remain your booty call. No, you can't do that. You have to establish the rules from the very beginning. If you have to hit it every two weeks to keep her satisfied, that's what you'd do in order to stay as option three," he said before I interrupted him. "What about option two, Unc, what does a guy do to become option two?" I said sarcastically. "Your ass may think this is a joke, but I'm trying to make sure you don't get caught out there and end up compromising your happiness because you feel the need to make some woman happy," he said with a serious tone. At first, I was trying to be funny and then I realized that what my uncle was saying had some truth to it.

My uncle grew up in a household where my grandfather was forced to marry my grandmother when he wasn't even ready for marriage. He married her because she got pregnant, but they never had time to find out if they truly loved each other. Their gunshot wedding was arranged by my grandmother's parents. He watched as they fought and bickered until they became old together. They never divorced, because they felt it would be too expensive for them, but they were never happy together. My uncle took that as a lesson and decided that he would try to find absolute happiness when it's time for him to get married, and that's if absolute happiness even exists. I was still waiting to find out the limitations of the second-option guy, and just when I thought that conversation was over, he busted out with, "Okay, the second option guy is the guy she'll call when she has a bad day. He's there to listen. He makes her feel special. He's attentive and he would go to the moon for her. She's not necessarily interested in him per se, but he can be good marriage material. She's not even willing to sleep with him, because she wants him to continue to think highly of her. Meanwhile, option number one is not emotionally there and she's hoping that he can make up his mind any day, so she can stop making booty calls to option number three who fucks her the way she likes to be fucked, but option number three is not worthy of marriage. I tell you, man, women have more game than men," was his final statement. The Fleet Center couldn't come soon enough. I wanted to start talking about sports. After parking the car at a lot located near the Fleet Center, we went in to watch the game. The Celtics put a whipping on the Bulls, less Michael Jordan. By then, Jordan had decided to hang up his shoes and the Bulls never looked like the championship team they once were when he was playing.

I enjoyed spending time with my uncle. We went and got some food after the game before calling it a night. I did mention to him that I was looking into starting a publishing company with the equity money that I pulled from my house. He encouraged me to do as much research as possible. As he knew it, I was flipping houses full-time. That was my story and I was sticking to it. My uncle didn't need to know that I worked as a gigolo.

Dirty Little Secrets

I always dreaded having sex with Helen, but I knew fucking her was essential to my lifestyle. The next day I had to make a special date with the "old prune," because the Boston Tops were playing; she just couldn't go alone. A new tuxedo was purchased, courtesy of her. I had to look my best when I stepped out with this woman. She paraded me around like a piece of meat and everyone knew that I was fucking her for her money. I felt like a dirty prostitute. However, Helen was very classy and she taught me a lot about business. She was a shrewd businesswoman who watched her husband's every business move- even when he thought she was paying him no attention. As a real-estate developer, her husband could've given Trump a run for his money. His company built most of downtown Boston and he owned a fifty percent stake of everything. Helen was sitting on chromes if I were to compare her assets to wheels on a car. Physically, Helen looked a little older than her actual age due to the excessive make-up she wore throughout her life. She wasn't so vain that she wanted a facelift, but Botox was a regular part of her beauty regimen. One time I showed up at her house to find her face looking completely stiff and her eyebrows arched up like she was permanently surprised. She wore that look for a couple of days before her face went back to normal. It was kind of scary having sex with her with that look on her face. I had no idea when she was coming or going.

I didn't meet Helen through the regular circle of people in Newton. I met her at a democratic fundraiser. My uncle who happened to be connected to the local democratic chapter in Boston took me to this fundraiser and I happened to meet Helen there. She seemed distant and people seemed to have been afraid of her. Her jewelry and wardrobe signified wealth and class, and lots of it too. I was dancing with her and one thing led to another and before I knew it, I became a kept man and this woman was taking care of me. Helen understood that in order to keep me, she had to pay me. I gave her no indication that I was seeing anybody else and I dared not bring anybody to the penthouse she gave me, as Helen had her own set of keys to it. She paid the cost to be the boss.

Helen's body was typical of a fifty-five year old except for her breasts. She had breast implants, but I wished she would have had a tummy tuck because she carried a kangaroo pouch like she was five months pregnant. Despite all my physical dislikes, Helen treated me fairly. Over time, I realized she was lonely and at the same time worried about the company she kept. She was in a position of authority where her decisions were crucial to the success of her business, and at the same time, many people were vying for her attention for the wrong reasons. She recognized that, too. My arrangement with Helen was probably the most comfortable for her, because she knew my purpose and she knew my price. I sometimes went out of my way to make her feel special, but she'd always tell me, "Dave, you really don't have to buy me flowers. I feel that only needy women who want to feel worthy are always looking for flowers from a man. Most of the time, they wither and die within a week, so what's the point? My husband never got me flowers because he knew that they couldn't make up for what he lacked and I loved him for that. You need to save your money otherwise I wouldn't be paying you to be here." She was blunt, but she was right. I had to think long and hard about her statement before I understood her point. I realized that flowers weren't really that special because they served no purpose, most of the time, other than to say 'I'm sorry.' A woman should feel special by the way her husband or boyfriend treats her, not by the amount of flowers he buys her after an argument. Even when the flowers are bought for no reason at all, there's always an agenda, because most men don't usually continue with the practice after they get what they want," she told me.

Helen was definitely a special lady, but I'll be damned if I didn't get frustrated with her dry pussy. It would take KY Jelly, Vaseline, and Baby oil to get through her dry canal. I often wondered why she even wanted to have sex with me. It seemed to be so painful. I knew that my dick hurt half the time. She used to wear nice lingerie that she had no business wearing. I would look at her in her high heels, fishnet stockings and a teddy and think to myself, "what the fuck?" She would walk into the room parading around like she was a sexy goddess; and I would have to find a way to get my dick hard to please her. She reminded me of Eartha Kitt in Boomerang. Somehow, she was majestically able to get my dick hard at the slight touch of her tongue wrapped around my dick. Helen was an expert at blowjobs. As long as my eyes were closed, I was able to imagine my dick being sucked by a much hotter woman, every time. The routine was to keep myself occupied in fantasyland while I maintained my erection with Helen. Turning the lights off was not an option, as she wanted to see me penetrate her. It was an ego boost for her to see that she could still turn on a young man. Her wrinkled skin, cellulite, stretch marks and the varicose veins were oblivious to her; but they stood out to me like a sore thumb. The closing of my eyes as if her pussy was heaven was my only way to imagine that Kelly or some other hot chick stood before me. She wasn't shapely at all for a sister and I could see why that white man found her so sexy. Helen was shaped like a white woman and was light enough to pass as one, but she revealed to me that she was black and her daddy was a light-skinned dude who used to run numbers in Boston. He slept with her mother while she was still married to her white husband. When she came out, they couldn't tell that she was a biracial baby, but she later found out that her daddy was black through a DNA test and her mother had to come clean. However, Helen lived her life as a white woman and met her husband while she was attending college.

I guess fucking me was Helen's way of giving the world the finger. She had lived all her life in secrecy and she grew tired of it. Since she was in a powerful position, she really didn't care what the rest of the world thought of her. She would show up at events with me on her arm and shock a room full of white people. However, what I liked best about Helen was that she took care of me. She wasn't frivolous with her money when it came to me. She made sure I led a good life. For the most part, I only received a twenty thousand dollar monthly allowance from Helen, but she would always take me shopping to buy me the finer things. I never had to worry about Caribbean or European vacations, clothes, fine dining and a top of the line penthouse. She gave me a penthouse suite in one of her buildings. Helen made my life sweet and beautiful, but my greed and need for pussy didn't keep me from fucking the other women. I also needed to be my own man in case the old lady cut me off.

I knew that I wanted to be there for Helen forever because I felt like I was the only friend she had, at times. I can't even say that my friendship with her was sincere because I benefited from her wealth as well. Honestly, there was no way in the world that Helen could be fucking a man like me regularly if she didn't have money. Helen took what rich men normally did and reversed it with me. My greedy ass allowed it because I sought a certain type of lifestyle. I also enjoyed the fact that Helen wasn't a pest. She was too busy running her company to bother me. I never thought about having a girlfriend because I didn't want to jeopardize my lifestyle. I had enough pussy during the day to the point where I didn't need to connect with anybody emotionally, so I thought.

That night when we got to Helen's house from the concert, I had no choice but to perform my duty. She went into the bathroom and came back wearing a lace teddy. Her veneers were shining bright as she flashed a smile thinking that her presence could get enough blood flowing to my limp dick. Kissing her was mandatory, because she enjoyed the intimacy. Surprisingly, Helen was a good kisser. I remember the first time I kissed her I expected her teeth to fall out of her mouth, until she told me they were veneers. Her teeth were just too perfect and I thought they were dentures. I was a little disgusted with the idea of kissing her, but as time went on, I found her to be a good kisser. We would kiss for long periods. After kissing and fondling her fake breasts, I always had to make my way down to her crotch. My mouth never produced enough saliva to get her pussy wet. I would lick her all night and I would not get a drop of moisture from her pussy even though she claimed to enjoy my oral skills. "You're a cunnilingus expert," she would say.

I tried to completely remove the thought of my mother in my head whenever I saw Helen. She was slightly older than my mom and that idea didn't sit well with me. As a matter of fact, my mom would be ashamed of me if she saw me with Helen. As a young woman, Helen was definitely gorgeous. I saw the pictures. However, she didn't age gracefully and her beauty probably started to fade when she was around age forty-five. Her husband was twenty years her senior when they married. I tried to glance at the picture of the younger Helen that sat on the nightstand while I ate her shaven pussy. I had requested that she kept her pussy shaven because I couldn't deal with the gray hairs. My imagination was my best tool whenever I was with Helen. As much as I enjoyed eating pussy, eating Helen's felt like a chore. I could hear her moaning and groaning as I took her clit in my mouth and started licking the expensive clit like my next meal depended on it. "Oh yes, you eat me so well," she said. Her drooping pussy lips had to be sucked and of course, I had to tongue fuck her. Fucking her with my tongue was a little easier because it was wet. "Yes David, you feel so good. Eat that pussy," she said. Helen's naughty side would only come out in the bedroom. Meanwhile, my dick was still limp. I sat on the edge of the bed while she knelt down between my legs to suck my dick. She was an expert at it and I could tell why she probably landed a billionaire. With my eyes shut tight, I sat back and enjoyed the maneuvering of Helen's tongue up and down my dick. She took the head in her mouth and made it something supernatural. I started humping her mouth and was actually enjoying it.

After laying the groundwork with my tongue and getting a blowjob from Helen, it was customary to have anal sex with her. She had grown accustomed to it because it was her husband's favorite and somewhere along the way, it also became a favorite of hers as well. After wrapping the condom tight around my dick, I started pouring baby oil all over Helen's ass and into her anus. My dick would always enter with ease and Helen seemed to have gotten off on it. I would fuck her ass for about fifteen minutes before moving on to her pussy. As I got ready to resuscitate Helen's pussy with my dick, I could see the downward slope taking shape on my penis. "No, this can't happen now. I need this erection," I yelled to myself quietly. I was losing it at the most inopportune time. I quickly shut my eyes and imagined "Buffy, the body" standing before me in her high heels. The blood flow suddenly returned. I reached for the container of KY Jelly after I wrapped my dick in an extra large Magnum condom. Almost a quarter of the bottle was rubbed around my dick before I commenced my penetration inside her dry walls. I really wasn't sure whether or not she was enjoying my strokes, but I continued to stroke her until more lubricant was needed. "Fuck me!" she blurted out. Her command might've fueled my dick because it suddenly got harder. I'm inside her pumping away while my finger rest atop of her clit. Under the night light in her bedroom, I could see every wrinkle and imperfection on her dated skin.

It took another five minutes of stroking her before she finally yelled, "I'm coming! You do such a good job fucking me." Mission was accomplished and I was done. She didn't really care that I didn't cum, and to be quite honest, I didn't really care that I didn't cum. My job was to make sure that she reached the skies and I knew every time I did that she opened up her purse, I mean her heart. The appreciation Helen showed me for a good nut was unheard of. Whether I was willing to admit it or not, I enjoyed being around Helen in close quarters. The wisdom and knowledge was always coming and I wanted to absorb it every time. I just wished that we could've hung out without the sex requirement, sometimes.

Sally

Life was going great and everything was fine. By then, I had close to twenty-five clients, earning more money in a month than most people earned in America in a year. I had my truck and my convertible Jag, a penthouse downtown Boston and more money in the bank than I could have dreamed possible. It was a perfect life. My routine for Helen was a twice a week outing and making sure she got some each time I saw her. I was comfortable enough with that. However, Sally was starting to become addicted to my dick and I was getting addicted a little to her freaky ways. Every time I saw her, we would push the envelope a little more, sexually. What was taboo at first became the norm to me. Tying her up on the bed, whipping her, peeing on her, fucking her while she hung from the ceiling on a sling and banging her ass out on the Stockade no longer thrilled me, or her. She started having me do more weird shit. Like the one time she had me wear a strap-on to fuck her. While my dick invaded her pussy, the strap-on was in her anus doubling her pleasure. "Oh shit, I like that. Give it to me hard," she begged. Her asshole stretched beyond imagination and I couldn't understand how this little frail looking woman could take on my big dick and an even bigger strap-on.

Sally was on her back on the table and my dick was all the way up in her when she suggested that I put my hands around her neck and squeeze. "This woman is really crazy," I thought to myself. I had never met a woman who was into asphyxiation before, so I was reluctant to participate. My fear was that I was gonna choke her to death. I was pounding her pussy, pulling on her nipple ring with my left hand while my right hand was wrapped around her neck. "Squeeze harder," she commanded as I tried to push one more nut out of her. I was fucking her with all that I had and felt like I could break this woman in half, but she was begging for more. I tightened my wrist around her neck as she turned beet red. She was shaking violently before I let go of her. "Why did you stop? I was having the best orgasm," she said. "I stopped because I was scared that I might've killed a white woman," I said jokingly to her. "Don't worry about it, I can handle it," she assured me. It wasn't the kind of assurance that I was looking for. That woman scared the hell out of me when her body erupted in this violent trance.

Sally and I decided to take a little break before going another round. As I sat there watching this woman, I was wondering what was going on in her mind that she wanted to be strangled during sex. Was there something psychologically wrong with her? Was there something wrong with me for allowing her to pull me into her little game? I really wished I could've seen her eyes, but the required blindfold kept us from making eye contact. The eyes really say a lot about a person. I guess I never wanted to know what was being said, because I made them all wear blindfolds. While I sat there looking dazed and thinking about the worse possible scenario, I felt the warmth of Sally's mouth on my dick. She was licking away and my dick was forever receptive. "Your cock is so big and beautiful, the ladies must love you," she said as she licked my dick. I could see the enjoyment on her face as she went from the shaft of my penis and down to my balls. With each lick, she was satisfying her own Mandingo fantasy. She struggled as she took my dick down her throat, but she didn't gag. She had become used to it by then. Mounting me was one of her favorite things. I was sitting with my legs spread and my dick reaching for the sky when she slid a condom on me and mounted me. For a woman so skinny, her pussy was deep. Up and down she went on my dick and I swore it was gonna come out of her throat. She turned around to face the wall while she sat on my dick. I was inside her doing damage, but she loved every minute of it. She reached for my hand and placed it around her neck again. My rhythm was good and I was doing a great job fucking her. Not paying too much attention to her, all I could hear was "Choke me." I was lost in her ass and in love with my own rhythm, so I squeezed as she asked. "Harder," she said again. Not realizing my own strength and determined to fuck this chick to submission, I started squeezing her neck harder. I never once thought about the discoloration on her face because I couldn't see her face. She wasn't facing me. It wasn't until I was busting my own nut that I realized I was fucking a stiff body.

Sally had lost consciousness while I squeezed on her neck, but because she wasn't facing me, and me being lost in my own performance, I never realized that I choked her until she passed out. At first, I just thought I could wake her up by throwing some water on her face. After I threw a glass of water on her face, she still laid there seemingly lifeless. Panic started to set in. I looked at her purple face and all I could think about was my great life disappearing before me. What the hell was I gonna do? I was gonna call Marsha to tell her, but I opted against it. I gathered my clothes, got dressed and got the hell outta there. I was hoping and praying that I didn't leave any evidence behind that could implicate me. I made sure I left no trace of hair, fingerprints or any other DNA evidence that could be used against me. My condoms and the wrappers were wrapped tight in a napkin in my pocket. I left the house through the back door hoping that none of the neighbors saw me.

Her death was eating away at my heart as I ran out of the house, because I didn't mean to kill her and I knew deep in my heart that I wasn't a killer. I was more upset at myself for allowing her to push me to take things this far. She was a wonderful person in her own way and didn't deserve to be killed, but I wasn't sure if I was ready to turn myself in to the authorities for a murder that I didn't willingly commit. It pained me to walk out of the house without calling the authorities, but no one would believe my version of what took place. It was a tough decision, but I decided to wait for them to come and get me. If the truth shall set me free, then they will get the truth from me when I'm caught.

Cindy

My worst nightmare came true when I saw Cindy on the six o'clock news telling a channel 7 reporter that she had seen a person go into the house. There was a possibility that I could be implicated in this murder, but even worse, they were saying that Sally was possibly raped also. All that rough sex we were having could've easily implied rape. Luckily, I was wearing a hoody, so she couldn't fully describe me. As discreet as I thought I was being, Cindy was even more discreet in the way that she kept tabs on the people who were coming and going in her neighborhood. She was the best neighborhood watchdog that Bingham Lane had ever seen. My freedom and my life were riding on her words. I thought about taking Cindy out as the only possible witness, but I wasn't truly a murderer. I killed by accident and I couldn't do it again. Even worse than that, I didn't want Helen to have any inclination that I was a murderer. For some reason, I always felt that Helen was always a little scared when she was with me. She didn't know enough about men like me to feel comfortable enough to let her guard down. I didn't know where to begin. I sat in the living room at my penthouse thinking that God was trying to get back at me for doing what I have been doing. I shouldn't have been sleeping with married women for money. I shouldn't have used Helen for money. I shouldn't have been fucking my friend's sister. I shouldn't have been doing this and I shouldn't have been doing that, was all that I could think about. That night, I got very little sleep as I anticipated the cops to breaking down my door to come get me at any moment. Every little noise made me jumpy and paranoid.

I woke up the next morning feeling tired and groggy only to find Cindy doing the talk- show circuit. She was talking about being a witness in the case. She was using the case for her own celebrity; and the media was giving her all the attention she sought. Just what I needed-another day of worry in my life, I thought to myself. I honestly didn't know what to do, so I decided to sit by and let the chips fall where they may. Before I could even do that, I saw the caption "Breaking News" on channel 7. "Police just reported that they have gotten a break in the possible murder case of Mrs. Sally Botticelli, a married mother of two children. A warrant may be issued as early as tomorrow for the arrest of the suspect," reported by the news reporter. The same caption appeared on every other station, I noticed this when I decided to surf through my cable channels. My back was against the wall and I felt the life being sucked out of me. I wish Cindy would take her ass somewhere and stop drawing attention to the case.

She was opening her big mouth and letting the world know, including me, that the guilty was not going to get away with murder. Why couldn't somebody put a muzzle on her? She needed to be shut up. I was scared. Her description of the man was vague enough that it could've been anybody my height and weight, but that was only what she revealed publicly. I had no idea what she said to the cops in private. I should've known that she would be sitting by her window watching what was going on in other people's lives because she had no life of her own. It was a well-known fact that her husband suffered from erectile dysfunction. She wasn't getting any, so she spent her time minding everybody else's business.

I didn't even know why I was getting upset with Cindy. She was only doing the neighborly thing by going to the cops to tell them about a possible suspect. I thought

I took every precautious measure to make sure I wasn't seen by anyone. None of my clients were supposed to divulge their appointments with anybody. I was so confident that my routine was working I started to let down my guard. I'm glad I parked a few blocks away from the house down at the Train Station.

Marsha

I called Marsha and I asked for her to meet me somewhere. Still upset over her friend's death, Marsha tried to tell me she couldn't meet me right away. I insisted and she continued to refuse me. Finally, I asked her to call me later when things settled down.

After I got off the phone with Marsha, I started going nuts. I felt like my mind was playing tricks on me. I interpreted her action towards me as an indication of guilt on my part. How dare she think I was guilty before I even got a chance to let her hear my side of the story, I thought. She sure as hell didn't act like this two nights ago when I was tearing her pussy apart while her husband was hard at work. My thoughts grew more sinister by the minute. I was starting to feel caged in and I hadn't even been arrested or charged with any crime yet.

Marsha had some nerve! Just three days ago, she invited me to the Holiday Inn in Dedham and for a two-hour romp. I gave her more pleasure in two hours than her husband gave her during the life of their marriage. She walked in wearing a shiny raincoat, boy shorts, bra and high heel pumps. All I could do was lick my lips when she dropped her coat to the floor. This Amazon of a woman was so sexy to me. With her body still intact from her daily exercise regimen, Marsha was the only woman I knew that could pull off wearing boy shorts and a bra and make it look so sexy at a size twelve. My dick instantly gave way as it started to reel its head through my pants for a possible invasion of Marsha's slippery terrain of pleasure. She placed one of her legs up on the bed exposing part of her crotch to me, pointed to it and said, "Get to eating." I had that look on my face whenever I saw Marsha and she just knew that I had to eat her pussy first, before we did anything. I bent down on my knees and inhaled the sweet aroma of her pussy before pulling her boy shorts to the side so I could taste her pinkness. Marsha must've been just as excited as me, because her pussy was apparently dripping wet and waiting for my tongue excursion.

First, I stuck a finger in her pussy, and then put it in my mouth. "You are so nasty and freaky," she said while enjoying every minute of my action. When my tongue made contact with her clit, she reached out and grabbed my hair for balance. Marsha knew that she would lose equilibrium the minute my tongue venomously attacked her clit. It pulsated a little in my mouth and I could feel it erecting from under the foreskin. I licked her clit slowly, back and forth and round and round. My index and middle fingers, meanwhile, searched for her G-spot. She started grinding on my face. I held on to her round ass to keep from falling on my back while my mouth was attached to her pussy. She started winding faster and grinding harder each time my tongue went into a circular motion on her clit. My fingers were all the way up in her and she couldn't stand it any longer. I reached deeper and pushed my fingers farther as she lost control. I held in my contempt, because only I knew how much I enjoyed pleasing Marsha.

Her legs started shaking uncontrollably as her juices neared her knees. She had reached the point of no return and she wanted to get back on the mountaintop. The second nut would be different and it would take her favorite tool to get her there. But first things first, Marsha enjoyed sucking my dick, and the pleasure was all mine as she sat on the edge of the couch while I stood before her with my dick standing freely as the long- awaited appetizer she longed for. She started with a little kiss on the tip as if it were her baby and then her tongue was soon wrapped around it as she tried to suck life into it. Marsha did a great job licking the sensitive part of my dick slowly with her tongue. Her wagging was efficient as she sent me into convulsions moments later. Pleased with her performance, she enjoyed taking my salty semen down her throat. She then came up my chest and started kissing on my nipples. My dick never wavered even after ejaculating a couple of ounces of thick protein.

Her flexibility baffled me as she raised one of her legs and placed it on my shoulder. I could see deep inside her pussy and my dick was hungry. She gave me no chance to reach for a condom as her pussy rubbed against my crotch. I took the tip of my dick and rubbed it up and down her clit. "Stop teasing me. I wanna get fucked," she said. She reached down and stuck my dick inside her, raw. Her pussy felt good and I didn't want to stop. I could see my dick going in and out of her with her legs stretched out against my shoulder. It brought a different kind of excitement. I stroked and pumped away at her pussy while my mouth was lost on her breasts. My dream of fucking a gymnast was being realized, but the difference was that Marsha could've never been a gymnast with her big frame, those women are tiny. "Don't come in me,' she pleaded. It was already too late because I was working on my second nut by then. Marsha had that affect on me. I could bust so many nuts with her it was unbelievable. She didn't even feel the brief softening of my dick because I continued to hump her even after I came. After regaining full erection, I set out to teach her pussy a wonderful lesson that she wouldn't soon forget.

I brought Marsha to the chair sitting on the corner of the room and I spread her legs open while I pummeled her pussy for the next half hour. Having busted two nuts already, I knew it would take some time before I busted my third and Marsha was more than happy to be the beneficiary to my performance. "I want it from the back," I said as she got up from the chair to turn around. Still wearing her heels, Marsha looked as sexy as a woman could be with her ass sticking out to me while her hands rested on the arms of the chair. I parted her cheeks symmetrically perfect as the mushroom head of my penis made its way inside her. I could see the pleasurable reaction from her each time I inserted my dick inside her. I kept taking it all the way out and inserting it back in. "I like that," she said. I know. By then, I was on my tippy toes trying to bust my third nut and hopefully taking Marsha on a fifth tour of seventh heaven. "Yes baby, that's it. I'm cumming again," she exclaimed, and so was I. She pushed back against my dick and I could feel my tip hitting her G-spot. I humped and stroked and humped and stroked until I damn near came inside her again, but I pulled out quickly for a back shot.

    That happened just a couple days ago, and now she was acting like I was a murderer. All kinds of shit were running through my mind and I felt that Marsha should've been my best support, at the time. I couldn't discuss my situation with neither Rammell nor Kevin. I hadn't seen them in a while because I was so busy doing these women. The last time I saw them, I lied to them about what I was doing for work. They both thought I was flipping houses because that's the lie I told them. They were impressed with my car, but I didn't make the time to chill with my boys. Of course, I also couldn't say anything because I was sleeping with Kevin's sister.

    Marsha finally called me a few hours later and she agreed to meet with me and talk. I had no idea what she knew, so I had planned to hear all that she had to say before I incriminated myself. I pulled up in the supermarket parking lot with my fingers crossed hoping that Marsha didn't sell me out to the cops. I know if she had any inclination that I had something to do with her friend's death, she would've turned me in to the cops. Why wouldn't she? It's hard to find anyone who would condone murder. I know I wouldn't, under any circumstance. I expected Marsha to basically tell me that she thought I was involved, but instead I found a crying and broken woman ready to move on with her life and was looking toward me for comfort.

"Hi baby," I said as she entered my car. A sobbing and teary-eyed Marsha leaned over to give me a kiss on my lips. "After what happened to Sally today, I think I'm ready to leave my husband. Life's too short for me to be living with an unhappy situation," she said. She threw me off with her statement. Marsha wasn't even on the same street as me never mind the same page. "I think I'm starting to fall for you and I want to know if there's any chance that we can be together," she said. I was thinking, "What?" "Are you sure you want to leave your husband?" I asked hesitantly and unsure. "I'm tired of his neglect, emotional abuse, cheating and disrespect. I want out. I'm not leaving him because of you, but I would like to date you after I leave him," she confirmed. Wow, I really allowed my mind to play tricks on me all day. I had no idea that Marsha was falling for me. She also revealed that she couldn't talk to me earlier because her husband was in her face and he was making her feel like shit. I was starting to lose focus. I needed to stay on track and I needed to make sure that my name would not come up as a suspect in the case. I was still worried about the possible warrant being issued. Anyway, I reached over and gave Marsha a tight hug. "Thank you. I needed that," she said to me.

While I sympathized with Marsha, I still had my life and freedom to worry about. "Do you have any idea what happened to Sally?" I asked curiously. "I'm not sure, but Cindy is doing everything she can to make sure the killer is caught. I think she's got a pretty good idea of the description of the murderer," she revealed. Her words were like daggers in my heart. It suddenly felt warm in the car and I had to put my window down. Damn! I'm going to jail, was all I kept thinking about. I needed to say something to Marsha, but I didn't know what to say. "Do you believe that she was raped like the cops are saying?" I cautiously asked. "I'm not sure, but there are also whispers that she had a sexual dungeon in her house. I really don't care. I just want justice for my friend and I want to leave my husband because life is too damn short," she said adamantly. "So where are you gonna go?" "I'm probably gonna go to my mom's until I can get an apartment. I've already called her and she said it was ok." "Well, if you absolutely need to, I have a two-bedroom apartment available in Hyde Park and it's yours if you want it," I told her. "This is what I mean about you, despite all that gigolo shit that you're doing, you're still sweet and that's what I like about you," she revealed. I needed somebody in my corner, anybody, it might as well have been Marsha. "You can call me later and I'll make arrangement to get you the keys," I told her. She gave me a long kiss before exiting the car.

My World Upside Down

Man, I had no idea that Marsha was falling for me. I was seeing her on a regular basis, and after a while, I think I started liking her, too. She was no longer a client; she had become a friend. I only had sex with her, because I thought that's what she wanted from me at times, but I never considered having that kind of relationship with her. I'm not saying that I didn't know I liked her, but I wasn't willing to give up my lifestyle just yet for her. I had gotten used to my penthouse, luxury car and having a lot of cash. Getting into a relationship with Marsha would stop all that. I know she wouldn't want me to continue sleeping with her friends for money. And what I worried about the most was Helen. She was my meal ticket and I couldn't tell her that I decided to take on a girlfriend who was married. Decisions? Decisions? I had to decide what to do, but first I needed to know which direction my life was headed.

I wanted to stop watching the news, but I couldn't because that was my only outlet to what was going on with the case. All the housewives had called me to cancel their appointments because of the media hoopla surrounding the case in the neighborhood. I also didn't want to go back to that area to confirm Cindy's suspicion. I needed the break anyway. The one person I couldn't take a break from was Helen. She had no idea I was involved in that case and she really didn't pay much attention to it. Women were being raped and killed everyday in the city, so there was nothing special about that case that would interest Helen. I had problems getting an erection with her before, but now with all that was going in my head, I needed Viagra if she was gonna get a rise out of me. Normalcy was a thing of the past and I needed to be careful, so that Helen didn't notice a change in my behavior. Whenever I was out with Helen, I was always looking over my shoulders. I expected the cops to show up and arrest me at any time.

An investigation into her finances revealed that Sally took out five thousand dollars every other week out of her personal account and the cops were trying to figure out why. Extortion was brought up and all kinds of other speculations. The case was all over the place and I was just hoping it didn't lead to me. The cops were begging anyone with information to come forward and cooperate. Meanwhile, the usual suspects were rounded up on trumped-up charges, brought to the police station for a lineup. Any black man with a criminal history of rape who fit that category was arrested. Cindy was the sole witness to the case and I was afraid that some innocent man was gonna go to jail for an accident that took place with me. The case dominated the local six-o'clock and eleven-o'clock news everyday. The media wanted justice. The police wanted justice, and the people wanted justice. Unfortunately, they would not get the justice they wanted. Cindy identified a young brother named Eric Drill befitting my description. He was charged with aggravated rape, first degree murder, breaking and entering, and extortion. I had no idea how they figured out those charges.

My conscience was eating at me because I knew the truth, but I didn't know what to do, still. A mob of people waited outside of the courtroom after the brother was arraigned and they wanted his head on a stick for killing a white girl. Bulletproof vest and special security had to be provided for this young man to keep the mob from getting to him. I wish that his arrest would bring relief to me, but it made me feel worse. His wrap sheet revealed that he had raped two women in the past, but he was able to beat the cases because there was no physical evidence to link him to the crimes. Third time could be the charm for the young man who seemed to have the worst luck in the world.

Eric appeared to be no older than me and his demeanor was calm and a little too laid back for a rapist. The only reason why the cops were able to pin this on him was that he had no alibi when the crime took place. He was a hustler and he happened to be home alone at the time of the crime. He didn't even use his cell phone to call anybody during the time. Tough luck! While I felt a burden might have been lifted off my shoulders, I felt bad that this dude was embroiled in this murder. I wish there was a way to get him off. Everybody hated him, but Sally's husband was especially angry and wanted this man sent off to prison for life. He probably would've killed Eric with his bare hands if he could. That asshole never even gave a damn about his wife, and now he was gong ho for justice.

One of the federal officers assigned to the case was a recent resident of Boston and a transfer from New York City. He was a single man assigned to special cases across the country by the FBI. He didn't seem to be convinced that the man charged with the crime was the actual murderer. His training convinced him that it wasn't an open and shut case as the local cops believed. Behind the scenes, he was doing his own investigation. Word had leaked that the housewives on Bingham Lane were being served by this gigolo and detective Raymond Barkley felt that there was a possible link between the gigolo and Sally. The last thing I needed was for some arrogant detective to feel that the case hadn't been solved. The only reason I found out this man was involved in the case was because the panicking housewives started calling me and telling me that he had been asking them questions about their finances. The patterns of withdrawals from their personal bank accounts were similar to Sally's. One more thing that I had to worry about, I thought. He left his card with Marsha. I immediately went to work to find out as much as I could about this detective.

Detective Raymond Barkley

Fresh off a case in New York and Atlanta, Detective Barkley was one of the best in his profession. A native of Brooklyn, New York, Raymond Barkley attended Massachusetts College of Liberal Arts, formerly known as North Adams State College. He worked undercover to crack a drug operation that was netting millions of dollars weekly in between New York and Atlanta. Detective Barkley was able to infiltrate the toughest gang of street thugs and risked his life to bring down Killer Ken and his empire. The Bureau figured he'd be the perfect guy to solve this murder case. Having been trained in various aspects of crime since joining the force a year out of college, Raymond Barkley had earned the trust of his subordinates at the bureau. I was just hoping that this guy was not hot on my trail.

Life for Eric as he knew it was about to get worse before it got better. While in custody for the brutal murder and rape of Sally, many other women came forward to disclose their own encounter with Eric. He had come close to killing many women after raping them. I was shocked. I never would've thought of that brother as a rapist. My chances of getting away with murder were looking better by the day, but I still had Mr. Raymond Barkley to worry about.

I learned that Raymond Barkley was one of those asinine officers who wasn't fulfilled until he saw a case through. This man would go to the end of the earth to get justice. His resume and accolades were readily available on the FBI website for those special people with access and I knew that I had to watch my steps with him. My uncle was connected and I had access to more information that most people. That's how I was able to look Mr. Barkley's file at the Bureau. The unexpected knocks on the doors kept coming, and each time, Mr. Barkley was curious about one more thing. None of the women cracked under pressure and they made it clear to Detective Barkley that they didn't want him jeopardizing their marriage. Of course, Cindy was more than willing to cooperate because she was one of the few women on that street who wasn't a customer of mine. The women had taken precautious measures to make sure that my entrance into their homes wasn't in full view of Cindy. There were times when I came through the window, side door, back door and rarely through the front door. When I did go through the front door, I was always in costume and my hat always shielded my face.

The best decision that I could've made was not allowing these women to see what I looked like. The blindfold worked perfectly because I remained anonymous to all of them. However, Detective Raymond Barkley was trying his hardest to expose my anonymity. Detective Barkley felt he might've found a weak link in Mrs. Riley. He kept knocking on her door, and she became more scared with each knock. "Mrs. Riley, I'm not here to ruin your marriage. What you do behind your husband's back is your business, but I'm here to discover the truth," Detective Barkley told Mrs. Riley who was sobbing uncontrollably. "The autopsy report on Sally revealed that she could've been possibly strangled by accident. I want to make sure I cover all my leads. This information has not been leaked to the media, so I'm gonna need your help on this," he told her. "I don't know how I can possibly help you. I have no idea who Sally was sleeping with and what her sexual habits were," she said through sobs. "Mrs.

Riley, isn't it ironic that most of the women on this street aren't willing to say anything, but all of them were withdrawing the same amount of money from the bank on different days. It's no coincidence and I plan to get to the bottom of it" he assured her.

Detective Barkley's angle was to scare the housewife into thinking that her secret would be revealed and she would bring shame to herself and her husband if she didn't tell him the truth. Mrs. Riley thought long and hard and decided not to tell him anything on that particular night. "Detective Barkley, unless you have a warrant for my arrest, there's no need for me to talk to you any more. I suggest you don't let the door hit you on your way out," she said while she headed to the kitchen.

Detective Barkley was a little upset that this woman was playing hardball with him. In fact, they were all playing hardball with him and he knew exactly how to get Mrs. Riley to cave. He figured an unannounced visit while Mr. Riley was home would seal the deal. No woman wants to be confronted with infidelity in front of her husband by another man, and Mrs. Riley sure as hell wouldn't be able to lie to her husband about an affair. It was one thing if he never found out, but if the affair was brought up, she couldn't lie about it. Detective Barkley discovered Mrs. Riley's weakness while talking to her. She couldn't look him straight in the eye and she played around with her hair the whole time, which suggested that she was lying. The other wives were pros at it and they gave little indication they would cooperate with him. Most of the other women wouldn't even allow the detective to set foot in their house. They were well aware of their rights and knew full and well that they didn't have to talk to him unless they were considered suspects in the case. Mrs. Riley didn't follow the rules and guidelines of the wives. A few of them were apprehensive about allowing her to be part of the pact from the beginning. Some brought up the fact that she could break under pressure and would one day confess to her husband about me, but they ignored their own advice and allowed her to join, anyway.

Detective Barkley knew that he only had one opening to the case and he had to pursue it full-force. There was no indication of a breaking and entering, but the local police charged Eric with that anyway. Detective Barkley figured that Sally knew her assailant. The dungeon in her basement especially left the overly-curious detective puzzled. Through conversations with her husband, Detective Barkley found out that the couple was very freaky and they sometimes went beyond normal borders with their sexual adventures. Mrs. Riley was the only person that could confirm what he wanted to know He wanted to make sure she told him what he needed to know even if he had to use illegal measures to get the info out of her. The possible threat of obstruction of justice was his next move and with a charge that carried a possible sentence of five years or more in prison, he knew that Mrs. Riley was going to buckle under pressure.

Mrs. Riley

Mrs. Riley only agreed to be part of the sexual charades because of the excitement it would bring to her life. Of all the wives that I slept with, she was the most boring. I wondered how such a boring woman could complain about her husband's cheating. I could see why the man had a girlfriend on the side upon first seeing her. I'm not saying that her drudging ways should justify his behavior, but he clearly needed to have another outlet to relieve himself of his stress. Still, he didn't have to treat her inhumanely.

I remember the first time I saw her. She was standing there with her back hunched, blindfolded and confused about what was to take place. Unable to see me because of the blindfold, she seemed a little too uncomfortable with our arrangement. I could see the confused look on her face even though her eyes were covered. She was the epitome of a plain Jane. The silky-looking, long nightgown, she wore made her look more like a Mormon. I tried my best to look beyond her discomfort because I was there to do a job. I reached out and grabbed her hand. "What are you doing?" she asked. "I'm just trying to ease the tension. You don't seem to be comfortable with this at all," I told her. "Well, I haven't exactly cheated on my husband before. This is all new to me," she revealed. It was so obvious that she didn't have to say anything. Besides, it would take someone earning a couple of grand to even sleep with her.

The impossible task of getting turned on by this woman was something that I definitely didn't want to think about. "Can we talk for a while?" she asked. "Sure.

What do you wanna talk about?" I asked curiously. "I don't know...tell me why you do this," she said. "Do what?" I asked. "Why do you go around sleeping with women for money?" She almost baffled me with her question. I really didn't have a logical answer, but I attempted to give her an honest one anyway. "Well, the money is good and I get to have fun in the process. Most of the time, I enjoy having sex with some of the women. I guess you could say it's exciting," I told her. "So there's no emotion on your part. Strictly business and that's it, huh?" she asked. "Pretty much. There's no reason to get attached to people that are married; that's what they have a husband for," I said impatiently. This woman was starting to act like a damn counselor and I didn't need to be counseled.

A few minutes later, Mrs. Riley handed me an envelope and said, "I think I'm gonna have to pass. I don't have what it takes to go through with this, but you can take the money for taking the time to come out here." I almost felt bad taking the money from her, but business is business and my time was money. I counted two thousand dollars. I gave Mrs. Riley a kiss on the cheek before heading to the door to make my way home. I sort of felt bad for her and I thought about her devotion to a cheating husband. He was the worst of all the husbands because he never took his wife anywhere. He treated her like she was his maid and rarely showed any affection towards her. Marsha told me that he was also physically abusive in addition to his psychological and verbal rant that she endured everyday. I really wished that she had gone through with it. A woman like her needed to be treated special even if it was just once in her life. Her husband hardly slept at home and he allowed his girlfriend to disrespect his wife. These people made it seem like a divorce was the hardest thing to go through. Life could've been much simpler had one of them just filed for divorce.

Walls are Closing in

The air around me was getting thinner everyday. I could see my beginning and my end. Sitting in my large living room, I could feel the steel bars in front of me. There was no kitchen, bedroom, dining room or bathroom. All I could see was this cramped place with one toilet and two bunk beds. My eyes were wide open, but I wasn't seeing what was in front of me. My mind was elsewhere and all I could see and hear were the voices of prisoners and wardens. The prisoners were spitting in my face while the wardens were laughing at me. What the hell is going on? I wondered. Marsha had just called to ask if I had anything to do with Sally's murder because Detective Barkley never let up about his questions regarding "The Bedroom Bandit." The whispers had turned to loud screams and my existence became a reality. The vow to keep me a secret had been broken and Mrs. Riley caved under pressure. The name "The Bedroom Bandit" was decided by the group, I later learned.

She revealed to her husband all of what was happening between me and the other women. She also got the beat-down of a lifetime for having been involved. Her face was black and blue and her husband didn't believe that she didn't go through with it, because she had given me the payment of two thousand dollars. He was more angry about the money, because she didn't get an allowance like most of the other wives. She was using his money. She was only allowed access to their bank account to go grocery shopping and purchase other household goods. Her husband was also pissed at her because their only child was born with down syndrome and he blamed her for it. They only married after she got pregnant because of his overly religious parents. There was never any love in the marriage, and a lot of anger because of his handicap son.

Detective Barkley had reached his intention; and Mrs. Riley revealed him as much as she knew about me. Putting a face to me was the next task on his "to-do" list. After hearing all that Marsha had to say, I asked her to come over to talk to me without thinking too much about it. I paced the floor back and forth in my penthouse going crazy out of my mind because I knew that the boys in blue were soon coming for me. The spacious, two thousand square feet luxurious penthouse, decorated with the most expensive furniture and lavish linen, was all a blur to me. All of it may soon be gone and traded for a single bunk bed with a roommate possibly named Bubba, who's gonna want to make me his bitch. The convertible Jag and all the pussy in the world will soon vanish. I couldn't live without pussy. My breaths were getting shorter. I needed ventilation. I was scared. I was about to pass out when I heard a knock on my door. It was a good thing that I had called the front desk earlier to tell them to allow Marsha access up to my apartment. She came just in time to keep me from passing out. She found a brown paper bag in the cupboard and she forced me to breathe into it. She then walked me to the sofa and placed a wet towel on my forehead while she tried her best to nurse me.

When everything settled down, I decided against telling Marsha the whole story of how Sally was accidentally killed by me. I didn't know if she would believe me because she only knew part of my character. After Marsha comforted me and helped me to regain my normal breathing, I felt a little better. In fact, I felt good enough to take her on my couch. I was sitting back with my head up and my eyes closed as Marsha pulled my dick out of my pants and took it in her mouth. I commenced an oral treat that was much needed. It had been a while since I got some good pussy and I needed to relieve my stress. I held on to the back of her head as she went up and down on my dick, soothing my every worry with tongue. I even humped her mouth a few times. "Suck it. I love the way you suck my dick," I told her. "I love sucking your big dick. It tastes so good," she replied. The restriction between the zipper and the limited amount of space to get her hand to the base of my dick near my balls forced me to pull my pants off altogether. I was sitting butt naked on the butter soft leather couch with Marsha now kneeling between my legs and sucking the skin off my dick. It felt good, and I enjoyed it for a while, but I wanted to eat her even more.

I think Marsha wore more dresses and skirts around me than she ever wore pants, that was a good thing, because it gave me easy access to her pussy. Her dress was soon pulled above her thighs and her underwear to the side as I slid a finger inside of her. "Ooh, that feels good," she cooed. I continued stroking her with my finger while standing above her with my dick in her mouth. Her pussy kept calling my name and before I knew it, I was laying on top of Marsha in the 69 position on the couch. She managed to get a grip on my dick while my tongue explored her clit. Another finger was inserted for insurance and Marsha started grinding wildly. I could always tell when she was coming because she would tighten up her body and lay still while the stress exited her body. After releasing her tension, she told me, "I want you to fuck me." Without much hesitation, I obliged. Marsha knelt on the couch with her hands resting on the back part of the couch and her legs spread while facing the wall. My dick was more than eager to penetrate her. Once again, I found myself going inside Marsha, raw. Her pussy felt so good. I started stroking her slowly while I palmed her ass cheeks. The speeds of my strokes were perfect. I was smacking her ass loudly. "Tell me you like this dick," I demanded while sweat poured over my body. The sound of my hand against Marsha's ass cheeks sounded like loud drums at an African ritual. Not once did I even notice or hear the movement of keys through the lock.

　　　　I was fucking Marsha hard when Helen opened the door to find my dick going in and out of Marsha's pussy, raw. "What the hell are you doing!" was the only thing I heard before I turned around to see Helen standing there looking angry as hell and ready to cut my dick off. "I want you and your floozy out of my house," she said angrily. I didn't know what to say as my dick went limp with shock. I was standing there frozen. I fucked up once more. "Get the fuck out of my house," she reiterated. I knew then that Helen never intended on giving me that penthouse as she had promised. Her promise was based on the fact that I had to continue fucking her and her only until her pussy couldn't stand a dick anymore. "I can't believe you're having unprotected sex with this floozy in my apartment." There it was, she confirmed it for me. She considered the penthouse hers. It seemed like I was frozen in time as I observed the devilish look on Helen's wrinkly face. "At least if you're gonna mess around, you should've made sure she was worth it, and not some cheap floozy," she burst out. "Bitch, you call me a floozy one more time and I will mop the floor with you," Marsha told her. I could see intimidation and fear in Helen's face after Marsha got up from the couch to head towards her. I had to quickly grab her to make sure she didn't go to jail for assault, because I knew back in the day Marsha was known for beating chicks down around the way.

I didn't know what to say to Marsha other than I was sorry. She already knew the deal with the penthouse, because I had told her about Helen. She gathered her things and walked toward the door to make her way out, but not before scaring Helen by acting like she was about to charge towards her. Helen took off to the next room and locked the door behind her. She thought Marsha was chasing her. After Marsha left, I felt like my world was tumbling down and everything I was doing was going wrong. Meanwhile, Helen kept going on and on and continued to make me feel like shit. I tried to gather as much of my belonging as possible before I left. Since all of my apartments were rented, I had no choice but to go back to my mother's house for a few days. It was a good thing that I bought the Jag in my name because Helen wanted to take that back, as well. I wasn't financially worried, though. I still had enough money in the bank to support myself, and my business plan to start my own publishing company was becoming a fast reality.

As I drove to my mother's house, I couldn't believe how stupid I had been to bring Marsha to the penthouse. If anything, Helen was connected enough in the city of Boston to make sure I stayed out of jail. I should've run to her first. She would've had my back. I never meant to hurt her, but what was done was done and there was no taking it back. I told her I was sorry before I left and she retorted with, "You are sorry. You're the sorriest man I've ever met." There was a limit to what I was going to allow her to get away with, and calling me sorry was the last straw. I charged toward her as if I was about to smack the hell out of her out of anger, but I caught myself and told her she wasn't worth it. I still had

to come back later to pick up my truck. I was hoping that
she didn't have the building manager void my access card
to the garage, and she didn't. She must've forgotten about
it.

More Problems

A month and half had passed since Sally's burial, and Detective Barkley was working hard at connecting the dots. Mrs. Riley had divulged everyone's business to him and he came up with the possibility that Sally had a lover who went too far with her during sex. Since no one knew me, it would be a task for him to connect me to the crime. Meanwhile, Eric was getting more than his share of coverage in the news. This guy was an habitual rapist who had mastered his trade. Many of the women he raped were too afraid to come forward because he had beaten two rape charges in the past and he threatened to kill them if they ever went to the authorities. Detective Barley didn't seem to be worried about him; he was already in custody. The local police and prosecutor were going to make sure that Eric never saw the outside world ever again. With five victims coming forward and counting, his days as a free man were numbered. Numerous other charges were brought up against him. He faced a possibility of 100 years behind bars, including another charge for the one crime he didn't commit, Sally's murder. Detective Barkley was more concerned about the criminal on the loose, which was the real killer.

I figured Detective Barkley would leave the case alone, but finding out the truth was more important to this relentless asshole than I thought. By then, I had settled into one of my apartments in Dorchester. I was trying to move on with my life, but I still had the monkey of Sally's death on my back.

I was home one evening trying to set up my home office for my newly formed company called Stories R Us Publishing when I received a call from Marsha. She was on the phone sobbing about how she would have to go back to her husband after leaving him because she found out she was pregnant. I ended up moving into the apartment that I offered to her because she didn't want to be a burden on me. She had been staying with her mom for the last six weeks. When I heard Marsha's revelation, my heart dropped. I remembered the time that I came in her. I waited a few minutes to see if she was going to ask me if I had anything to do with her pregnancy, but she had more going in her life than to worry about me. "I can't believe that I got pregnant. I can't even recall the last time I had sex with my husband. I don't want to have a child for this man. I'm not even happy with him. I may not have a choice," she said through sobs. I wasn't gonna volunteer myself as a possible dad just yet, but she needed some kind of comfort. "Well, if you decide to have the baby and still leave him, I will always be here for you," I told her. I could hear a little relief from her voice on the phone, but I knew my words weren't enough to make her feel better about the situation.

While sitting there on the phone talking to Marsha, I knew that there was no way in the world, if that baby was mine, her husband wouldn't be able to tell. We looked completely different, and if that baby looked anything like my family, it would be very obvious. I couldn't afford to take on any new problems, but they kept piling up. "You know, I'm trying my best to get on my feet. I went and got a job and I want to do this on my own. I don't want my husband to control me anymore. I can't go back to him. I need to figure out what I want to do about the baby," she said resignedly. Either Marsha hadn't done the math in her head, or she completely forgot about our encounter. I didn't want to add to an already complicated problem, so I kept my mouth shut. However, in the back of my mind, I knew that I came inside Marsha and there was a possibility that she was carrying my baby. There was no way to be certain about it until the baby was born. So I decided to play the "wait and see" game. Meanwhile, I vowed to be there for her and offer support in every way possible before we hung up the phone.

I hated growing up without my father and there was no way that I would do that to my child. Though my life was in turmoil, I needed to make provisions for the baby just in case I had to go to jail or if I had to make a decision to be with Marsha. Either way, I was going to be a man about it. I was excited about the possibility of becoming a dad. I would do everything differently than my father. My son or daughter would grow up proud. I even started thinking about being with Marsha. It's not as if I didn't like her. I really liked her.

During the few weeks that I stayed with my mother, I hardly saw Kelly. And when I saw her, her man was always within the vicinity cutting his eyes at me like he knew what was up. I couldn't tell whether or not she was happy, but she seemed to accept her situation. We never had a chance to have a conversation other than casual greetings. I just hoped that her man was taking good care of her. She deserved it. I also never led on to my mother regarding the happenings and drama in my life. She asked how my business venture was coming along and how I was able to afford such an expensive car, I lied to her. I stuck to my story about flipping houses. I was consistent across the board with everybody. I even lied to Rammell. I didn't want to be connected to that murder in any possible way.

As time went by, I also started to care less and less about what Kevin would think if he found out I was sleeping with his sister. Already deeply rooted in the streets, because he had lost his job at UPS a few years later when he got caught smoking weed. The only thing he could possibly do was kick my ass. And that he would have to do everyday because I would keep fighting him until there was no fight left in me. A baby was lot more important to me than my friendship with Kevin. I was hoping he would understand that I would want to take on my responsibilities as a father and be there for his sister. But the way my life was going, who knows?

Just when I thought my problems were piling up, there was one more thing that I didn't see coming. While I was chilling at my house one evening, my doorbell rang. When I went downstairs to open the door, I was ambushed. A group of angry men attacked me. I didn't even have chance to throw a punch as the angry mob pounced on me. "You think your dick is gold, huh? Take that," said one man as he kicked me in the rib cage. One of them could hardly breathe right, but he was able to punch me in the eye while two of his partners held me down. I got my ass whipped that day and the ambulance had to take me to the hospital. Luckily, my neighbors upstairs discovered me moments later and called the ambulance.

When it was all said and done, I had a broken neck, two broken arms, a broken foot, fractured ribs, two black eyes and facial lacerations. I heard the doctor say that there was a chance that I would not make it because of internal bleeding. My eyes may have been shut, but I could hear all that was going on. Those men went to work on me. I didn't know who I was going to turn to or what to do after my recovery. I thought about my uncle, but I was afraid that he might reject me completely. My mind was still sharp through it all and I could still remember those people who were closest to me. Rammell was not an option on my list of people to call because he would be shocked that I went over the line and slept with Marsha. Rammell and I always talked about trust and staying away from each other's family members when it came to sex and relationships. Kevin would probably add to my injuries with a punch or a kick or two to my face, so that only left my mother as an option.

My Poor Mom

Of course, my mother hurried to the hospital when she heard about the incident. I could see the tears falling from her eyes as she sat on the chair in the corner of the room. Even though I couldn't talk or respond to anything, I could see and hear everything. Her only son almost got beaten to death and the details of the incident weren't clear to her just yet. The rumor was that I had been stealing money from people. At least, that's what was told to the cops because a few people heard the words spoken from the men who had beaten me up. It was a hard truth, but I knew my mom wanted confirmation. A part of me was hurting inside as I stared at the only woman who ever loved me unconditionally, my entire life. I never once thought about her when I was doing my dirty deeds. Maybe if I did, I wouldn't be laying on a hospital bed in pain and wondering what was going to become of my life after I left the hospital. My poor mother didn't deserve that. She worked hard all her life to make sure I was raised decently with morals. I failed her miserably and I was ashamed of myself.

Even in my most embarrassing moment, my mother was the only person who wasn't ashamed to claim me as her son. Word had spread around fast enough about the case. I feared that all those people that I worried about knew everything that I didn't want them to know. I honestly thought that my beat-down came courtesy of the angry husbands who found out that I was fucking their wives. None of the people I worried about cared enough to show up at the hospital to see me. At least, that's what I thought the first few days when I was laying there. I later found out that the hospital would only allow my mom visitation rights because my injuries were thought to be graver than they actually were. My mother held daily vigils and nightly prayers that I would make it. I already knew that I was gonna make it because I could hear what the doctors were saying about me. If half of my body wasn't wrapped up in a cast, I would have reached across the bed and slapped the silly taste out one of the doctor's mouth for having my mom think that I was not going to make it.

My uncle, Rammell, Kevin, Kelly and a few family members came by to see me. I was always happy to see them, but I couldn't say much to them or show any emotion. It was as if I was physically dead. I don't know why I couldn't just open my mouth to speak. I felt like my body was being controlled by something else. I couldn't even shake my head to acknowledge people's presence.

I especially remember my mom's prayers, "Dear God, he's the only son that I have. Please don't take him away from me. I don't know what he has done wrong, but I know you're a forgiving God, and you're gonna give him one more chance regardless of what he did. I really don't know what I'd do without him. There's a good side to him, God. He means well and he loves his family, please let him live," she prayed on and on and on. I figured God was trying to teach me a lesson. Why else would he allow all this crap to happen to me? My mother would force my visitors into sudden prayers for me. My mother was a devout Christian and God's number one servant. Why would he want to see her in pain? I wasn't even worried about me anymore. I hurt more knowing that my mother was in so much pain. Though almost comatose, I was still trying to come up with a new plan in my head, silently, to build my life, and make my mother proud. I thought about settling down with Marsha to try to raise our kid together as a family and developing my business. I thought about getting involved in my community to help the younger kids make better decisions. I thought about going to church regularly after leaving the hospital. I thought about telling my mother I loved her every time I saw her. I thought about calling Kevin to apologize for violating his trust. I thought about how I was gonna work hard to earn my uncle's trust again. I thought about how I was gonna be a good son to my mother and a good father to my child. I wanted to own up to my responsibilities. I wanted to tell Marsha that I impregnated her. I thought about some of these things while I watched my mother sob over me at the hospital.

　　　Whatever silent prayer my mother was reciting to herself must've worked, because my body started to respond to the medication and the doctor announced to my mother that I was gonna pull through. I wish I could give her the thumbs up to reassure her, but I couldn't raise a finger. My mother may have been praying to God on my behalf, but she had a lot to say to me, too. "Junior, I know you can't hear me right now, but I just want you to know that I'm not mad at you right now. I just want you to come home. I want my baby to live. I went through so much to give you a better life, and I worked so hard to make sure you didn't turn out like many of the young men on our block. I'm not disappointed in you and I don't ever want you to think that I am. However, I am angry, Junior. I'm angry at the fact that I've always told your father that we didn't need him, and that my son would be fine without him. I'm angry that you didn't make something more of yourself. I'm angry that you chose a path that you were not familiar with or used to, you had positive people in your life. I'm angry that you never realized that you're my special child. I'm angry that you disappointed your uncle.

I'm angry that I have to hear your name being smeared by people who don't know you. I'm angry that you're not responsible. And I'm angry that you don't realize how your actions can hurt so many people who love you." She spoke to me even though she knew I couldn't hear her.

Delirium

I must've been hallucinating to think that I was getting my ass beat by a mob of angry husbands. It took me a long time before I realized that there was no way in the world the women's husbands could find out who I was. My mind wasn't right and I was scared. I knew for certain that Marsha wouldn't reveal anything to her husband about me. She hated him too much and she was starting to care about me a lot. I had to figure out who ordered that beat-down against me. My incoherence led me down all kinds of wrong paths and my mind continued to play tricks on me. My mother was still sitting in the chair in the corner of the room, silently praying for my recovery even though the doctors had confirmed that I would recover completely. The casts around my arms and legs were bothersome because I kept itching and I couldn't scratch the itch. I tried my best to relax and took the medicinal air of the hospital into my nostrils. After I started to calm down, I realized that the unthinkable had just taken place. My beat-down was ordered by Helen, a sudden revelation brought on by my delusions.

I was knocked down so quickly when I was attacked, I couldn't even recall the faces of the men who jumped me. However, as I was laying there, dormant, I could hear one of them say, "This is for lady H, asshole," before spitting on me. There was only one woman that I knew with the initial H in her name. I couldn't even fathom a classy lady like Helen would send a bunch of goons after me. It was unthinkable and she was just too nice and classy to do such a thing. Upon my release from the hospital, I had nothing but time on my hand after my recovery process began at my mother's house. She took great care of me and nursed me like I was her baby all over again. I could see the pain that I caused to the only woman who loved me more than life itself. I made a promise to never do anything stupid to hurt her again. It seemed like I was everything that she had left in the world, but I never realized that until now.

My mother was able to go to my apartment to grab my laptop for me. My arms may have been in a cast, but my fingers worked well enough for me to use my computer. I was able to get online using my T-Mobile wireless card while I was at my mother's house. The goal was to find out everything I could about Helen and her husband. I learned that Helen's husband was the infamous Franco Renaldi, one of the biggest real-estate developers in Boston. However, he wasn't just a real-estate developer, he was also tied to the mob. Earlier during his rise to the top of the real-estate market, Mr. Renaldi paid the mob for many favors, including the clearance to buy some of Boston's prime real estate. He was forever indebted to them and after he died, his wife continued with the ties.

I researched old articles on the family, but Mr. Renaldi was too powerful to get convicted in court. My innocence led me into the arms of a mobster's widow. Helen had special people who looked out for her and those people were the same ones she sent after me to teach me a lesson. I figured they must not have wanted me dead or else I wouldn't still be alive. Then, I started hallucinating again wondering if they thought that they had killed me. Would they want to come back and finish the job? I wondered. Was I placing my mother's life in jeopardy by staying with her? Oh shit! I was scared out of my mind after I learned of this woman's connections. What the fuck was I gonna do? I thought about packing my shit and leaving the state, but where was I going? I loved Boston. I was paranoid as hell from then on. Every little noise had me running to the window to look for a Cadillac with tinted windows. I was going nuts out of my mind.

I had people visiting me everyday and each time someone came, I thought it was one of the mobsters coming after me to finish the job. I would try to keep Kevin, my uncle or Rammell around for as long as I could as company because I felt safe in their presence. Most of the time, I could see they were annoyed and ready to go home. I would go into diatribes about nothing just to keep them seated. I think they felt sorry for me and stuck around because of that. I never once revealed my fear to any of them.

The Family

I wasn't sure if my mom was able to figure out how delirious I was, but I was trying my best to keep it from her. Meanwhile, she was planning a cookout to celebrate my recovery. It had been eight weeks and I had the casts removed from my legs and arms. I walked around using a cane as support. Everybody was invited to the cookout, my friends, family and a few strangers who stopped by with some friends for the free food. It was my mother's way of celebrating life, my life. She had almost lost her only son and she wanted to make sure I was celebrated. I saw people that I hadn't seen in years, but I was most happy to see my uncle, my best friends and the look of happiness on my mother's face.

There was plenty of food and the DJ kept everyone entertained throughout the night. There was a particular gentleman who showed up that I had never seen in my life before. His mother was a cousin of my mother and uncle. He had just moved to Boston from New York and my mother wanted him to get acquainted with his family in Boston because he was living in the city alone. His mother had called to let my mother know he was in Boston. She asked my mother to welcome him and let him know that we were his family. This tall, dark, and handsome dude seemed to be a little older than me. He was more around my uncle's age. My uncle and he were talking like long, lost, best friends. After I was introduced to him, I found out that he used to come to Boston to spend the summer vacation with our family when he was younger. We shared the same maternal grandparents. His mother had migrated to New York, but she kept in contact with the family and she would send her son as a youngster to Boston to keep him away from the troubled streets of Brooklyn. His name was Cousin Ray Ray. There was something mysterious about him. He walked with authority and seemed to be able to read people well. He could sense all the bad elements at the party and he put my uncle on alert.

Cousin Ray Ray was cool and we talked about my situation. He talked to me almost as if he was a cop, maybe a detective even. It was almost as if he was doing investigation to learn what happened to me. I gave him some information, but I kept the crucial parts of what happened to myself. I was introduced to this dude as my cousin, but I didn't know him like that to be telling him my business. After talking to Cousin Ray Ray, I hopped and skipped my ass around to thank everyone who came to the party. I could see Cousin Ray Ray whispering something into my uncle's ear, but I didn't know what it was. However, I did see my uncle hug him in a congratulatory way like he was proud of him.

The party was over around one o'clock in the morning, but Cousin Ray Ray stuck around until the end like he was some sort of security. I talked to him for a few minutes and learned that he had just moved to Boston from New York to work on a project for some company, but he didn't go into details. He seemed like a cool enough dude, so I invited him to a Red Sox game along with my uncle the following weekend. The Red Sox happened to be playing the Yankees and Cousin Ray Ray was a diehard Yankee fan.

Moving Ahead

The Monday after the weekend of the party, I decided to go back to my apartment. I was almost one hundred percent and I needed to focus on my life and setting forward the plans for my publishing company. Even though the company was registered as a business and business cards were printed, website was underway and everything was in place, I still had no books to publish. I didn't know how to go about getting authors to submit their work to my company. Not only that, my company had no history as a publishing company. What I initially thought was going to be an easy task, proved to be a lot harder. After weeks of posting emails on different social websites requesting submissions, I grew frustrated and decided to pen my own story. I didn't know where to begin because I was not a novelist by trade, though I graduated college with a Bachelor's Degree in English. I also knew how to tell a story, according to my professors back in college, and I had one hell of a story to tell.

While sitting around in my apartment, I started to toy around with the story of a young man who was a drug dealer, but ended up in a war with his own brother because he didn't want to live in his brother's shadow anymore. I was almost twenty pages into the story, thinking everything I was writing was original, before Kevin told me he was reading a great book, Blood of My Brother by this husband and wife team of authors named Zoe and Yusuf Woods. The premise was the same as mine, but their story was already published and the story was off the chain. I finally made time to read the book series and both books are off the chain, just as Kevin said. I had to scrap my plans and go back to the drawing board. I went online and did some research of my own and found that many of the stories I was thinking about writing were already written; written by authors locked up in prison who found their voice in this new literary genre called "Street Lit." I was inspired and disappointed at the same time. I was inspired by the fact that these men committed themselves to writing stories about their lives that could potentially keep other young people from repeating their mistakes. I was also disappointed with the fact that some of these books glorified street life and drug dealing and there was no lesson to be learned from some of them. I read enough of those book to know that my book had to be different from what was already out there. I wanted to introduce my readers to something fresh.

I pondered my story all week and came up with nothing. It wasn't until I met up with my uncle and cousin Ray Ray for the baseball game that I figured out what I needed to write about. While we were at the game watching the Yankees put a beating on my beloved Red Sox, I started thinking about my own personal story. My journey from the time I was a little boy to my current situation. I knew that most people think that they have an interesting story to tell, but I felt mine was different. It was different in the fact that I endured a lot of pain from my interaction with women. I had allowed them to take control of my life. Also, the fact that I might have to go to prison for a murder that I didn't even commit willingly would add great suspense to it. I thought of myself as innocent and guilty at the same time. I was guilty for actually choking Sally to the point where she died, and innocent for participating in something that she wanted me to do. Of course, there was a lot more to my story as well that would make it all the more interesting. I had to figure my angle on the whole story.

      I found out that cousin Ray Ray was a trip. He still kept me in the dark about what he did for work and I started referring to him as Tommy from the show Martin. No one knew what Tommy's profession or job was and he could never explain it. My uncle might have known what Cousin Ray Ray did professionally, but he sure didn't lead on to what he knew. He was laughing right along with me every time I made a joke about Ray Ray. By the end of the game, the Yankees had beaten the Red Sox with a score of 15 to 9 and Ray Ray had more jokes than Eddie Murphy. He was cracking on our pitcher, talking about the Bambino curse and the lack of black players on the Red Sox roster since Jim Rice. The Red Sox, however, would go on to win the World Series that year. I had fun hanging out with the fellas, but I still thought about the problems awaiting me in my personal life. I walked around with a big Army knife in my car and carried it around whenever I needed to walk somewhere, even to the house from the car. I wasn't taking any more chances. The next time someone tried to jump me, I had planned to take at least one of them out.

Revelation

Marsha had made the decision to leave her husband for good and she was nearing birth with her baby. She was the most beautiful woman that I have ever seen pregnant. Her skin radiated and beauty shone. I was surprised when she came up to my apartment unannounced one day. Marsha was never the kind of woman to wear a lot of makeup. When I opened the door to see her face caked up with makeup, I knew something was wrong. She tried her best to cover the black eye and other bruises on her face caused by her husband, but I could tell underneath it all, she had been beaten. Uncertain whether the baby she was carrying was mine, I was still furious. Somebody needed to teach that fat bastard a lesson. How dare he put his hand on a pregnant woman? "What happened to your face?" I asked after I opened the door for her. "What do you mean?" she asked, trying to act dumb. "What do you mean what do I mean? I'm talking about your face being all black and blue. You're dark skinned but you're not that dark and that dark makeup you're wearing is not becoming," I said with obvious anger in my voice. I could tell she was trying to be careful with her words by the amount of time she took before answering me. "I slipped and fell down the steps at the house." She lied to me. "What, you slipped and fell on your face and nothing happened to the baby? Look, if you're gonna come here and lie to me, you can just leave because I'm not going to entertain that shit," I told her.

Marsha was not familiar with that tone coming from me and she knew she had better start telling the truth. "Okay, Hubert found out about you and he took it out on me," she revealed. "Found out about me, what are you talking about? You and I were always careful," I said. "I guess we weren't careful enough because he had pictures of us together kissing and doing things we shouldn't have been doing, according to him," she said with tears running down her face. I was trying to figure out the origin of her tears. I wondered if she was crying because she was caught or if the situation with her husband had deteriorated to the point where she just didn't want to be bothered with him anymore. I pulled her towards me for a hug, but her protruded stomach was in the way. I stood behind her, wrapped my hands around her stomach for comfort, and stared rubbing her belly. I wanted to know the whole story. "I want you to tell me what happened," I said to her while holding her. She grabbed my hand and led me towards the sofa. "I'm gonna be completely honest with you and I don't want you to be mad at me," she said. I was looking at her and thinking to myself that this woman may possibly be carrying my child, and I might have to take care of her, what can she possibly tell me that would make me mad? As far as I knew, Hubert's days with her were over and I wanted us to move forward with our lives. There was no way I was gonna let her go back to that goon, under any circumstances. I was thinking that Kevin and I should pay him a visit for a little payback. He needed to know what it felt like to be pounded on.

I sat on the couch next to Marsha waiting for her to tell me what happened. I could tell she was very emotional, so I tried to make her feel at ease by rubbing my hands on her back. "Well, you already know the story about how Hubert and I met. I know a lot of people think that I got with him because his family had money, but that's not the case at all. I got with Hubert because he was kind, generous, attentive and romantic, unlike any other man I had ever dated. I was able to look beyond the aesthetics because I liked him as a person. I grew to love him over time, but after we got married, he started to change. He was never great in the bedroom and I figured I could live with that because he did other things to satisfy me," I interrupted her to ask, "Does he eat pussy better than me?" I already knew when she said he did other things to satisfy her she was talking about how he ate her pussy. She had casually mentioned that in the past, but my ego wanted to confirm that my tongue game was up there with my dick game. I waited for an answer, but she didn't give me one. The smile on her face, however, was enough of an answer for me. It was also my way of bringing a smile to her face. She continued, "After we got married, Hubert became very selfish and most of the time, he wouldn't even eat my pussy. Mind you, this man came every time his dick met my pubic hair. If there was a 'second man' Hubert would be it. He lasted less than thirty seconds every time we had sex. I talked to him over, and over about my lack of satisfaction in the bedroom, but he never gave a damn. We were supposed to go see a sex therapist to help him with his early withdrawals/premature ejaculation problem, but his ego got in the way. And then, you came along. After I met you, it seemed like I was going through a rebirth. I agreed to have you service my friends because I didn't want to get attached to you. I was trying to create a safe haven for myself, but my emotions wouldn't let me. I became more distant with Hubert and I wouldn't let him touch me anymore. He started to become physically abusive and I was even more turned off by him. All I could think about all day was you. I also started to realize that Hubert also didn't want me to work all these years because he was afraid that I would one day meet a man who could satisfy my sexual needs. I agreed to stay home, but I was bored out of my mind, most of the time," she said this with tears streaming down her face. I could feel her pain. I reached my arms around her shoulders for a tight hug.

Against her better judgment, Marsha had returned to her husband after she found out she was pregnant. But I knew that she didn't want to be there. Now more than ever, I was hoping she was carrying my baby. I don't think Marsha ever once thought that she could be carrying my baby. I still hadn't told her that I came in her. From what she told me, it seemed like all Hubert was doing was watering her grass. He never got to plant anything. The chance of that baby being mine was really great. I wanted to hear the rest of the story, so after hugging and comforting her for a few minutes, she continued on, "Where was I? Oh yes, I was telling you how his insecurities kept me home and how I was bored at home. Anyway, after I met you, I started to develop true feelings that I never knew I had. The anticipation of seeing you, the touch of your hands against my skin, your breath against my face, the taste of your lips, your understanding, your friendship, your sexual prowess, all of it swept me off my feet. I wanted you and only you. Since I wasn't having sex with Hubert, he wanted to find out who I was having sex with. He hired a private investigator to follow me around. I had no clue that I was being followed, but when he showed me the pictures that the PI had taken of me and you, I told him the truth. I told him that I wasn't happy and I wanted out for good. He went ballistic and started beating the crap out of me and afterwards, he knelt down and said, 'Lady H, you know I didn't mean to hurt you. I can't afford to lose you blah blah blah...' I didn't wanna hear it. I'm ready to leave him."

I know she didn't just say he called her Lady H. I needed to confirm what I heard. "Did you just say he called you Lady H?" I asked. "Yes, that was his special name for me. My middle name is Hilda cause I was named after my grandmother and his name being Hubert, he called me his special Lady H," she said. A light bulb went on in my head and I got the solution to something that was bothering since I left the hospital. It was Hubert, not Helen, who sent those goons after me. After he found out she was messing with me, he sent his goons to teach me a lesson or may be even kill me to keep me away from her. That fat bastard had it coming. It was time to get even. I explained everything that happened to me to Marsha and she confirmed that he used to brag that she'd never be able to see me again. Marsha didn't know I had gotten beat up because I had stopped calling her when she decided to go back to that fat bastard. Everything was clear to me now and I had to make my moves clear. It was time to play chess.

Loving Marsha

I had never made love to a pregnant woman in my life, but the excitement that overcame me after I found out that Hubert was responsible for my beat-down was enough for me to be at ease. Suddenly, I wanted to make love to Marsha. The fear of the Italian mob was lifted and now I knew who my enemy was. I was free. I could always look into Marsha's eyes and determine whether she wanted me. At that moment, she didn't just want me, she needed me. I suddenly started to notice her radiant beauty and sexy pregnant body as I looked beyond the bruises on her face. This woman was in love with me and I started to fall for her as well. Her piercing eyes were on me the whole time as I unbuttoned her bra to expose her breasts that had grown to a D cup, due to the pregnancy. I took her lips in my mouth as my hand fondled her breasts. Her bra was a hindrance, so she decided to help me out by taking it off and throwing it on the floor. Mmmm, I said at the thought of sucking her breasts. I needed her kisses. I continued to rub my tongue against hers and sucking on her sexy lips ever so gently while she lay across my couch. Though twenty pounds heavier because of the baby, Marsha was as sexy as ever. I started to caress her breasts while she sucked on my fingers. I alternated between left and right and even brought them together in my mouth before I made my way down her belly towards her crotch.

Her pussy was nice and wet at the touch of my fingers. I tried to connect with her g-spot while my tongue created wonderful fireworks with a clit. I wanted to savor her taste in my mouth. Her moans and groans became louder as my tongue took over her pussy. I parted her lips with my tongue as it made its way inside her. I stuck it in and out of her and she held on to my head. "Eat me, baby. Nobody eats pussy as good as you," she said, revealing the answer to the question I had asked her earlier. Ego boosted and a need to satisfy her became stronger as I sucked on her pussy lips lightly. I knew her weak spot was her clit, so I surrounded it with my tongue, forcing her to hold my head tight between her legs until she climaxed all over my face.

Satisfied with her first orgasm, Marsha reached out for her favorite toy and placed it in her mouth. I was nine and a half inches deep down her throat as she slashed my dick with her tongue. "Oh shit!" I said as I held on to her head to allow her full access to my dick. I was losing control. She took it out and used her hand to massage the tip while moistening it with her spit. It worked. "Oh shit, baby, I'm coming," I announced. She stuck it back in her mouth, giving me the pleasure to soothe myself in a warm place. After I came, Marsha went to the bathroom to spit out the extra protein. I guess she was being careful because of the baby.

Walking to the bathroom, I was looking at her phat ass and my dick wanted more. I couldn't wait for her return. After freshening up, Marsha came back to find a hard dick waiting to please her. "Come here. I want you on the dining room table," I told her. Everything on the table was thrown to the floor to make room for Marsha to get on her back. Her pink pussy sat on the edge of the table as I penetrated her slowly. I kept my strokes soft, afraid to leave a knot on the baby's head with my hard dick. "I want you to fuck me harder, baby," she begged. "You sure? I don't wanna leave no knot on the baby's head," I told her. "The baby will be alright. Fuck me," she commanded. I obliged. I started stroking Marsha harder. I was fucking the hell out of her like I hadn't had pussy in years. Sweat started pouring down my body, but her pussy kept calling me. Pregnant pussy felt the best, I thought, as I stroked Marsha to ecstasy. "Oh shit baby, I'm coning again. Right there, don't stop," she instructed. Her right leg rested on my arm, which gave me complete penetrable access. I humped and stroked and grinded until she came once more.

　　　　I needed to make sure I busted my nut. I held both of her legs straight against my chest and hugged them until I fucked her to a nut. I was exhausted, but Marsha's pussy felt good. We would continue to fuck almost four weeks before the baby was born. By then, I had set up the baby's room and Marsha was set to move in with me.

Kevin

Kevin was a hothead, but he had also become a pothead. Weed was his way of life and hustling was how he earned a living. Though I didn't agree with his lifestyle, I was about to become part of his family and I needed to tell him the truth about me and his sister. I also wanted Kevin to help me teach Hubert a lesson for beating on Marsha. I knew exactly where to find Kevin. I drove up Selden Street and he was sitting there in the schoolyard with a group of dudes doing what became part of his daily life, smoking weed and talking shit. There must be a heightened, intellectual, elevated stimulus in weed, because Kevin was a lot more philosophical when he was high. The foul scent of malt liquor and weed crowded my nostril as I let the window down on my truck to talk to Kevin. "Can we go for a ride? I need to talk to you," I said to him. He turned to one of his homies and said, "Yo, I'll be back. Shorty coming back for that twenty. Take care of that for me." I knew what he meant but it was none of my business that he was selling drugs. Kevin also knew better to bring any drugs on him while riding with me. As he hopped in the truck, I noticed the chrome .45 around his waistband. I knew it was a non-negotiable issue because Kevin didn't go anywhere without his gun. I didn't even have to ask if he had drugs on him, because I knew he kept his stash in the schoolyard somewhere.

He hopped in the car and I started driving to nowhere. I just wanted to talk to him and let him know that I wanted to be with his sister and I was willing to step up to the plate and handle my business. I took one last look at the silver plated .45 before I began speaking. I wasn't sure what Kevin's reaction would be. "Kev, I know we ain't as tight as we used to be, but I wanna tell you that I still appreciate your friendship and we'll be friends forever," I told him. I knew that shit sounded a little mushy but I wanted to get it out the way. "Yo, I know you ain't getting soft on me, right? What's on your mind, kid?" he asked. Before I could respond, he continued, "It ain't like you just checking on a brother just to be checking. You know I got your back. You like a brother to me, so shoot." "Man, I don't know how to say this, man, but your sister and I are gonna be together," I said while waiting for a reaction. "What? That's what you gotta tell me? My sister is already at the house bragging about you to my moms. I just never said nothing. I was waiting for you to come to me like a man, but I know you a good dude, though. I ain't trippin'. You got my blessings, just treat my sister right. It ain't like you like that fat bastard who think he better than my family. I never liked his fat ass anyway," he revealed. Kevin had just given me the opening I needed to secure a serious ass whipping for Hubert. All I needed was to add fuel to the fire.

      "Yo, talking about dude, I got my personal beef with him, but more importantly, I need you to know that he was beating on your sister and I ain't really ready to let him get away with that shit," I told him. "What? That motherfucking fat bastard put his hand on my sister? Oh fuck that, we gotta teach his ass a lesson," he said angrily. "And he did that shit while she's pregnant, can you believe that?" I said with a little bit of contempt in my voice. "Yo, let me ask you something, is my sister's baby yours?" he said, changing the subject. "To be honest, I don't know, but it don't matter, cause she's with me now and I gotta be a father to her child," I told him. "That's what I'm talking about. Welcome to the family, fam," Kevin said while giving me dap. "So what we gonna do about fat boy?" I asked him. "Yo I'ma take care of it. You gotta a child to worry about. Don't get your hands dirty," he said. "Man, I wish it was that easy. I got to get my hands dirty. That bastard was the one who put me in the hospital. I found out he sent his goons to jump me," I told him. "Word, he did that shit. Yo, we gotta get that chump. But I don't think you should get involved, though. Me and my dawgs can take care of it. Don't worry, you gonna be happy with the results. He didn't have to get his hands dirty with you, why should you get yours dirty with him?" Kevin said. He made an excellent point. I decided to stay clear of the situation and allowed Kevin to handle it.

As I was driving him back to the block, we talked about the publishing company that I was about to start. Kevin was one of those smart dudes without a clue about his talent, but when I mentioned writing books to him, his eyes lit up. I knew he had enough imagination to come up with his own version of a story depicting "street life," so I was a little enthused when he told me that he would think about writing a book. He had seen enough shit on the street to write his own personal testament. I encouraged him. I drove back to the block and let him out the car. Before he exited, he gave me dap and said, "Welcome to the family, fam," once again.

Life Goes On

Despite all the drama that was happening in my life, I still had to go on with my life. As planned, Marsha moved in with me before giving birth. We didn't know what she was gonna have, so I decided to paint the room yellow and most of the clothes we bought for the baby were yellow. Marsha also told all her little rich friends who came to the hood for baby shower to buy things that were neutral colors because she didn't know what she was having. The sadness of Sally's death had come and gone and the ladies were moving on with their lives. I didn't stick around for too long at the baby shower because the women pretty much took over. I was happy and ready to be a dad, regardless who was the biological father.

I also had one more thing to think about, this pest of a detective was still going around harassing the ladies to find out who I was and what I looked like. No one was able to give him the information he wanted. Marsha had stopped taking his calls after she moved out of Hubert's house. I was still afraid that I might end up going to prison. I was surfing through my television channels when I came upon yet another breaking news caption. I always paused whenever I saw the caption "Breaking News" and this time would be no different. "There has been a new revelation surrounding the death of Mrs. Sally Botticelli, the woman who was found strangled to death. It has been reported that a rapist as originally thought, did not strangle Sally, according to the police. An FBI agent working the case was adamant about finding the real killer. A warrant has been issued for a new suspect in the case. However, the original suspect, Eric Drill, will remain in custody, and will be charged with numerous rape allegations brought forth by his victims. We'll continue to update you as the story develops. Stay tuned to NBC for more details," said the anchorwoman.

All I could think that I was finally caught. They finally figured out I was the murderer. I left a note in my top drawer with directions for Marsha to go to the bank to withdraw money from one specific account for the baby as well as a handwritten will and testament assigning everything I owned to my mother and how she was to help Marsha financially if I landed in prison for life. I made no phone calls to anyone. I simply waited for the cops to bust my door down and take me in. Meanwhile, Marsha was out with her mother getting more things for the baby. I never even bothered calling her, because I didn't want to ruin her day. I had fallen asleep on the couch and awoken by Marsha when she got home. She startled me when she tried to shake me. I thought the cops had finally come and I was screaming, "Ok, you got me. I give up." "I got you doing what?" she asked with a puzzled look on her face. "Were you having a bad dream?" "I was, honey." I pulled her towards me for a hug and a kiss. The television was still on and the six o'clock news was about to start. I didn't want Marsha to find out about the situation on the news, so I turned off the TV. However, I still wanted an update on what was going on.

I walked to my office and turned on my computer to watch the news live because it was streamlined online. Marsha knew whenever I walked into my office; it was because I needed to do work. She didn't even bother me. I used my headset to keep her from hearing anything. "Now a follow-up on the story we brought you earlier about the Botticelli case. Police now have confirmed that an arrest has been made in the case. The latest information we received is that Mr. Botticelli killed his wife after purchasing a five-million dollar insurance policy naming himself as the sole beneficiary. The police are reporting that the coroner's office said that Mrs. Botticelli was killed around seven o'clock on the evening of her murder. I knew I didn't kill her because I left her house at three o'clock that afternoon. I continued to listen to the newscast. "A videotape of Mrs. Botticelli having sex with a black man while wearing a blindfold was also found in Mr. Botticelli's possession. The police are reporting that the woman passed out briefly during sex with the man, but was later killed that evening by her angry husband. We'll have more on the story on the eleven o'clock news on channel 4 NBC news," the anchorwoman reported.

I had never been so relieved in my entire life. I knew I wasn't no killer. When Sally passed out, I panicked. I thought she was dead and bolted outta there. Now I knew the cops would be looking for me if they had a tape of me and Sally having sex. It was time to come clean with Marsha before lawyering up to go to the police station. I sat her down and told her everything, and explained every detail. I told her how scared I was and how Sally was always forcing me to push the envelope with her. I had no idea her sick husband had installed a hidden video camera in the basement. His own evidence took him down.

I showed up at the police station with my lawyer for my interrogation/interview. Since I already knew that they had a tape of me having sex with Sally, I just had to tell them the truth, the whole truth and nothing but the truth. The officers promised that my name would not be revealed to the media and my affiliation to the case would be kept to a minimum if I cooperated. My lawyer made sure everything was guaranteed in writing before I opened my mouth to say anything. The shocker in the case was that Mr. Botticelli videotaped himself choking his wife and the cops used it as evidence to convict him for the murder. Thanks to some FBI agent named Bradley, I was a free man. He received credit for solving the murder case, but his face could not be shown on camera because he was used for undercover assignments all over the country. His voice distorted during his television interview as well as his face hidden from the viewers.

No one understood the pain that I went through the last few months, worrying about my freedom and where my life was headed. I had no solid plans because of the uncertainty that lied ahead at the time. I decided that I would change my life and sleeping with women for money would be a thing of the past. I only needed one woman and Marsha was it. It was time for me to sit back, relax and welcome my new baby to the world.

A Beautiful Life

I finally had peace in my life. The cloud over my head was gone. My mother was happy that God didn't take me away and she was going to be a grandmother. I had a special lady in my life and most of all, my baby girl was born. I had the biggest baby at 12 lbs. I was watching the way the doctors were pulling her out of Marsha's vagina and I almost cried. People thought they were tears of joy, but I was crying because she was stretching my shit too big. That shit will never be as tight as it was before, but I was happy I had a healthy baby girl. I'm no DNA expert, but that baby came out looking just like me. Her eyes were glowing and big like mine and her feet, which is one of those family heirlooms that has been passed down from many generations, were as fat as any baby who were ever born in my family. My mother knew right away she was her grandchild, because she remembered what I looked like when I was born. I know that most people think that all babies look alike, but I beg to differ. My baby looked just like me. I put in enough work to make sure she came out looking like me.

My entire family was at my house to welcome my baby home. Congratulations came from everyone and in different forms. Some people gave us plain cash, while others handed envelopes with money and some brought clothing items for the baby, but everyone was happy for us. I was especially happy when my uncle told me he was proud of me. He was the one person that I wanted to make proud because he had been there for me. My mother was gonna be proud of me, regardless, because I'm her child. She didn't have to say it. I could see it in her eyes, just like I could see that the baby was mine through her eyes.

Meanwhile, Hubert wasn't having such a good day on the day my child was born. Kevin and his boys, dressed in black hoodies, black jeans and sneakers, made sure Marsha was the last woman Hubert ever laid his hands on. He had no idea why he was getting his ass whipped as Kevin and his boys kept it silent while they pummeled him. He was lucky he made it out of the hospital alive almost ten weeks later. I had to use a cane for a while after I came out of the hospital, but Hubert would be wheelchair bound for the rest of his life. Now being close to an invalid, the only thing he was hoping for was that my daughter would be biologically his and that Marsha would go back to him. No one would want a wheelchair bound fat, abusive bastard. When he knew he wasn't gonna win her back, he decided to ask for a blood test to find out if the baby was his. By law, he had the right to a blood test because he was still married to Marsha. My daughter had been home for almost ten weeks by then and I grew closer to her everyday. I was not ready to lose her to Hubert, but we had to do what was mandated by the court system. We went into court and they took swab samples from the baby, Marsha and the fat bastard. I was fuming inside because I didn't want to subject my baby to no blood test.

While we waited for the result of the blood test, Marsha also filed for divorce. She wanted nothing but her name back from him. She didn't need anything from him. Besides, I had planned to take my publishing company to the top of the industry. My family's future was solid.

I prayed to God everyday that my daughter was biologically mine. I knew that Hubert would be the biggest pain in the ass if that child turned out to be his. I would watch her at night while she slept and dream of a world of good for her. I enjoyed feeding her, burping her, changing her diapers and playing with her. I didn't want that to be taken away from me. I wanted to be the father she needed. As far as I was concerned, she was already my little girl and I didn't need a DNA test to make it official. I had accepted her as my own and since Marsha lived with me, I was going to be raising her, anyway. I also knew that I couldn't deny Hubert his right as a father, if he was proven to be the biological one. My daughter, named Savant, was going to have two dads if the test proved Hubert to be the biological father. I named her Savant because she was a learned person. We needed to learn too much about her before she was even assigned a last name. I wanted her to have my last name, but I couldn't do that yet because Marsha was still married and we didn't know if she was biologically mine, which didn't matter to me.

The result of the test finally came in the mail six weeks later. Marsha held the envelope in her hands as a stream of tears rolled down her cheeks. "I want you to promise that you will treat her as your own even if this test says she isn't," she said to me. She must have been out of her mind. That child was mine from the time she popped her out of her coochie. I was the one at the hospital watching her give birth to her. "Of course, she's mine. You shouldn't even question that. I will always love her just the same," I promised. "I also want you to know that I'm hoping to God this is your child because there's nothing more I want in this world." By then, her eyes were flooded. "Go ahead, open the envelope, baby," I told her as I crossed my fingers behind my back.

I closed my eyes for a few seconds and sighed as she broke the seal on the envelope. She opened it and there were quite a few pages in there. She went to the line that read, "There was no possibility of paternity," and a smile flashed across her face. I knew we had gotten some good news. It was official, Savant was my biological daughter and Hubert was assed out. I never wanted to see that asshole ever in my life again. The next time I saw him would be when he had to sign the divorce papers to finalize the divorce to Marsha who had by then become my fiancée. He was shocked to learn that she wanted nothing from him. His money was worth nothing to her.

Marsha and I were blessed to have the kind of outcome that we wished for. Not too many people in life get their prayers answered. We decided we were gonna take things slow. Marsha was the one who finally helped me figure out what my first book should be about. She said, " Since me and my girlfriends came up with the name 'The Bedroom Bandit' for you, I think you should write a book about the ordeal you just went through. I think there's quite a few ladies out there who would like to know the story of 'The Bedroom Bandit' That sealed it. I was no longer racking my brain for a book idea. 'The Bedroom Bandit' was the first title published by my company, Stories R US Publishing. Marsha became my marketing and promotional director, Rammell was director of sales and operation and, Kevin penned one of the best street novels ever written. We rode our way to the top. Marsha was right there with me back in the suburb living in a big house with our daughter, as a family. My book sold enough copies to make the New York Times Best-Seller List as well as Essence and the National Best-Seller List.

Kevin couldn't walk the streets without someone stopping him for an autograph. He became a celebrity after penning his first street novel. Rammell continued to bang every chick with a dream of becoming a writer he met at literary functions. Hopefully, he'll find his special someone one day.

The End

PS: To learn more about the character named, Ray Ray, please check out my book series titled, Sexual Exploits of a Nympho I & II.

NEGLECTED SOULS

Motherhood and the trials of loving too hard and not enough frame this story...The realism of these characters will bring tears to your spirit as you discover the hero in the villain you never saw coming... Neglected Souls is a gritty, honest and heart-stirring story of hope and personal triumph set in the ghettos of Boston.

In Stores!!!

Jimmy and Nina continue to feel a void in their lives because they haven't a clue about their genealogical make-up. Jimmy falls victims to a life threatening illness and only the right organ donor can save his life. Will the donor be the bridge to reconnect Jimmy and Nina to their biological family? Will Nina be the strength for her brother in his time of need? Will they ever find out what really happened to their mother?

In Stores!!!

Betrayal, lust, lies, murder, deception, sex and tainted love frame this story... Julian Stevens lacks the ambition and freak ability that Miko looks for in a man, but she married him despite his flaws to spite an ex-boyfriend. When Miko least expects it, the old boyfriend shows up and ready to sweep her off her feet again. She wants to have her cake and eat it too. While Miko's doing her own thing, Julian is determined to become everything Miko ever wanted in a man and more, but will he go to extreme lengths to prove he's worthy of Miko's love? Julian Stevens soon finds out that he's capable of being more than he could ever imagine as he embarks on a journey that will change his life forever.

In Stores!!!

The police in New York and other major cities around the country are increasingly victimizing black men. The violence has escalated to deadly force, most of the time without justification. In this controversial book, noted author Richard Jeanty, tackles the problem of police brutality and the unfair treatment of Black men at the hands of police in New York City and the rest of the country.

In Stores!!!

Just when Darren thinks his relationship with Tina is flourishing, there is yet another hurdle on the road hindering their bliss. Tina saw a therapist for months to deal with her sexual addiction, but now Darren is wondering if she was ever treated completely. Darren has not been taking care of home and Tina's frustrated and agrees to a break-up with Darren. Will Darren lose Tina for good? Will Tina ever realize that Darren is the best man for her?

In Stores!!

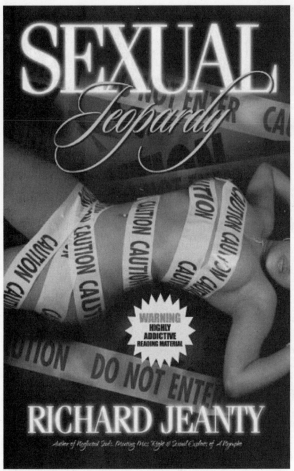

Ronald Murphy was a player all his life until he and his best friend, Myles, met the women of their dreams during a brief vacation in South Beach, Florida. Sexual Jeopardy is story of trust, betrayal, forgiveness, friendship and hope.

In Stores!!!

Tina develops an insatiable sexual appetite very early in life. She only loves her boyfriend, Darren, but he's too far away in college to satisfy her sexual needs.

Tina decides to get buck wild away in college

Will her sexual trysts jeopardize the lives of the men in her life?

In Stores!!!

Faith Jones, a woman in her mid-thirties, has given up on ever finding love again until she met her son's best friend, Darius. Faith Jones is walking a thin line of betrayal against her son for the love of Darius. Will Faith allow her emotions to outweigh her common sense?

In Stores!!!

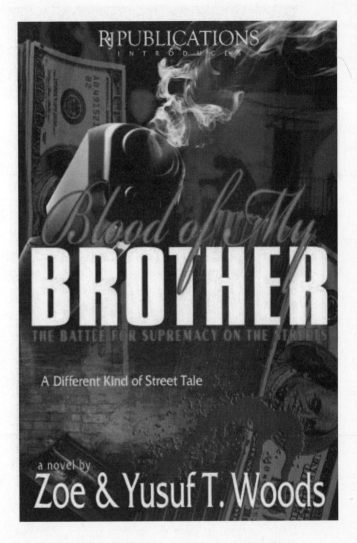

Roc was the man on the streets of Philadelphia, until his younger brother decided it was time to become his own man by wreaking havoc on Roc's crew without any regards for the blood relation they share. Drug, murder, mayhem and the pursuit of happiness can lead to deadly consequences. This story can only be told by a person who has lived it.

In Stores!!!

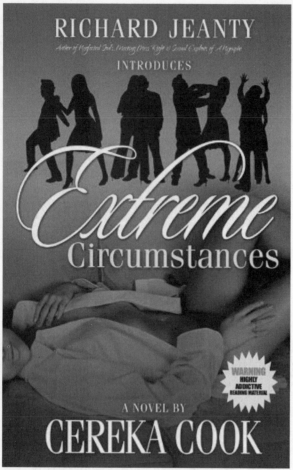

What happens when a devoted woman is betrayed? Come take a ride with Chanel as she takes her boyfriend, Donnell, to circumstances beyond belief after he betrays her trust with his endless infidelities. How long can Chanel's friend, Janai, use her looks to get what she wants from men before it catches up to her? Find out as Janai's gold-digging ways catch up with and she has to face the consequences of her extreme actions.

In Stores!!!

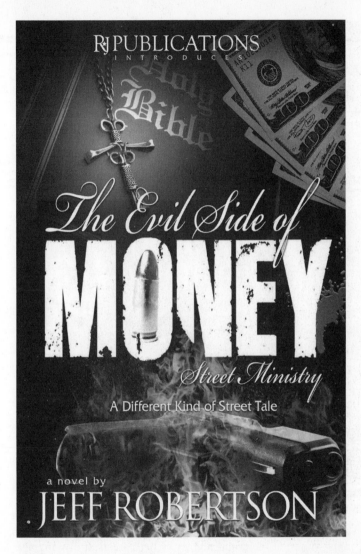

Violence, Intimidation and carnage are the order as Nathan and his brother set out to build the most powerful drug empires in Chicago. However, when God comes knocking, Nathan's conscience starts to surface. Will his haunted criminal past get the best of him?
In Stores!!

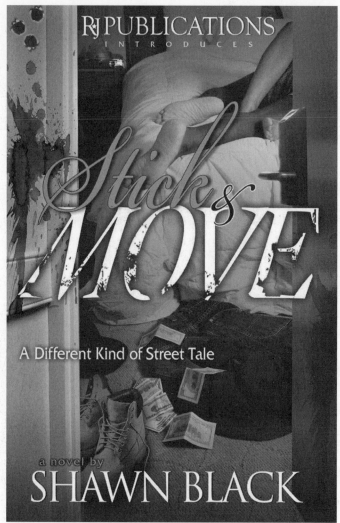

Yasmina witnessed the brutal murder of her parents at a young age at the hand of a drug dealer. This event stained her mind and upbringing as a result. Will Yamina's life come full circle with her past? Find out as Yasmina's crew, The Platinum Chicks, set out to make a name for themselves on the street.

In stores!!

Ashland's mother, Bianca, fights hard to suppress the truth from her daughter because she doesn't want her to marry Jordan, the grandson of an ex-lover she loathes. Ashland soon finds out how cruel and vengeful her mother can be, but what price will Bianca pay for redemption?

In stores!!

Malcolm is a wealthy virgin who decides to conceal his wealth
From the world until he meets the right woman. His wealthy best
friend, Dexter, hides his wealth from no one. Malcolm struggles to
find love in an environment where vanity and materialism are
rampant, while Dexter is getting more than enough of his share of
women. Malcolm needs develop self-esteem and confidence to meet
the right woman and Dexter's confidence is borderline arrogance.

Will bad boys like Dexter continue to take women for a ride?

Or will nice guys like Malcolm continue to finish last?

In Stores!!!

What happens when a woman's devotion to her fiancee is tested weeks before she gets married? What if her fiancee is just hiding behind the veil of ministry to deceive her? Find out as Sean Mitchell takes you on a journey you'll never forget into the lives of Angelica, Titus and Aurelius.

In Stores!!

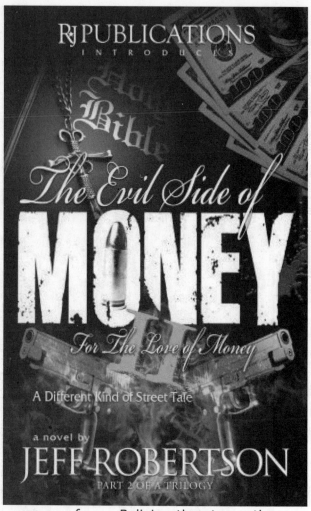

A beautigul woman from Bolivia threatens the existence of the drug empire that Nate and G have built. While Nate is head over heels for her, G can see right through her. As she brings on more conflict between the crew, G sets out to show Nate exactly who she is before she brings about their demise.

In Stores!!!

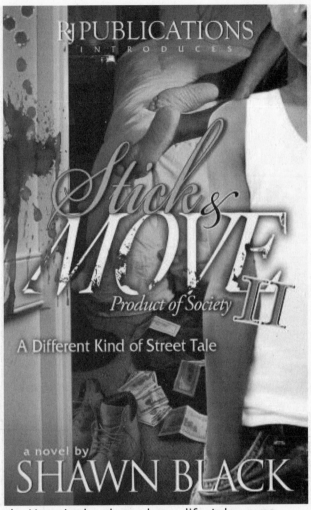

Scorcher and Yasmina's low key lifestyle was interrupted when they were taken down by the Feds, but their daughter, Serosa, was left to be raised by the foster care system. Will Serosa become a product of her environment or will she rise above it all? Her bloodline is undeniable, but will she be able to control it?

Coming April 2009!!

After Chasin' Satisfaction, Miko finds that satisfaction is not all that it's cracked up to be. As a matter of fact, it left nothing but death in its aftermath. Now living the glamorous life in Miami while putting the finishing touches on his hybrid condo hotel, Julian realizes with newfound success he's now become the hunted. Julian's success is threatened as someone from his past vows revenge on him.

Coming June 2009!!

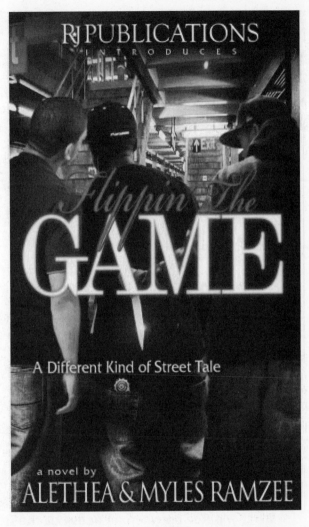

An ex-drug dealer finds himself in a bind after he's caught by the Feds. He has to decide which is more important, his family or his loyalty to the game. As he fights hard to make a decision, those who helped him to the top fear the worse from him. Will he get the chance to tell the govt. whole story, or will someone get to him before he becomes a snitch?

In Stores!!!

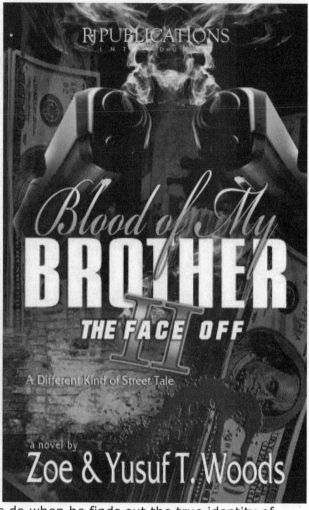

What will Roc do when he finds out the true identity of Solo? Will the blood shed come from his own brother Lil Mac? Will Roc and Solo take their beef to an explosive height on the street? Find out as Zoe and Yusuf bring the second installment to their hot street joint, Blood of My Brother.

In Stores!!!

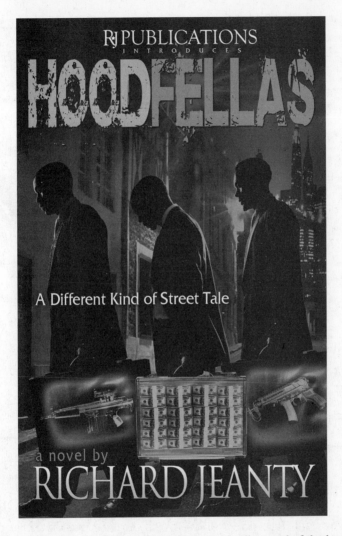

When an Ex-con finds himself destitute and in dire need of the basic necessities after he's released from prison, he turns to what he knows best, crime, but at what cost? Extortion, murder and mayhem drives him back to the top, but will he stay there?

In Stores !!!

What happens when someone falls insanely in love? Stalking is just
the beginning.

Coming May 2009!!!

PUBLICATIONS
BRINGING EXCITEMENT, FUN AND JOY TO READING

Use this coupon to order by mail

1. Neglected Souls, Richard Jeanty $14.95
2. Neglected No More, Richard Jeanty $14.95
3. Sexual Exploits of Nympho, Richard Jeanty $14.95
4. Meeting Ms. Right's Whip Appeal, Richard Jeanty $14.95
5. Me and Mrs. Jones, K.M Thompson ($14.95) Available
6. Chasin' Satisfaction, W.S Burkett ($14.95) Available
7. Extreme Circumstances, Cereka Cook ($14.95) Available
8. The Most Dangerous Gang In America, R. Jeanty $15.00
9. Sexual Exploits of a Nympho II, Richard Jeanty $15.00
10. Sexual Jeopardy, Richard Jeanty $14.95 Coming: 2/15/ 2008
11. Too Many Secrets, Too Many Lies, Sonya Sparks $15.00
12. Stick And Move, Shawn Black ($15.00) Coming 1/15/ 2008
13. Evil Side Of Money, Jeff Robertson $15.00
14. Cater To Her, W.S Burkett $15.00 Coming 3/30/ 2008
15. Blood of my Brother, Zoe & Ysuf Woods $15.00
16. Hoodfellas, Richard Jeanty $15.00 11/30/2008
17. The Bedroom Bandit, Richard Jeanty $15.00 March 2009
18. Stick N Move II, Shawn Black $15.00 April 2009
19. Miami Noire, W.S. Burkett $15.00 June 2009
20. Insanely In Love, Cereka Cook $15.00 May 2009
21. Blood of My Brother III, Zoe & Yusuf Woods August 2009

Name_____
Address_____
City_____State_____Zip Code_____

Please send the novels that I have circled above.

Shipping and Handling: Free
Total Number of Books_____
Total Amount Due_____

Buy 3 books and get 1 free. This offer is subject to change without notice.

Send institution check or money order (no cash or CODs) to:
RJ Publications
PO Box 300771
Jamaica, NY 11434

For more information please call 718-471-2926, or visit www.rjpublications.com

Please allow 2-3 weeks for delivery.

PUBLICATIONS
BRINGING EXCITEMENT, FUN AND JOY TO READING

Use this coupon to order by mail

22. Neglected Souls, Richard Jeanty $14.95
23. Neglected No More, Richard Jeanty $14.95
24. Sexual Exploits of Nympho, Richard Jeanty $14.95
25. Meeting Ms. Right's Whip Appeal, Richard Jeanty $14.95
26. Me and Mrs. Jones, K.M Thompson ($14.95) Available
27. Chasin' Satisfaction, W.S Burkett ($14.95) Available
28. Extreme Circumstances, Cereka Cook ($14.95) Available
29. The Most Dangerous Gang In America, R. Jeanty $15.00
30. Sexual Exploits of a Nympho II, Richard Jeanty $15.00
31. Sexual Jeopardy, Richard Jeanty $14.95 Coming: 2/15/ 2008
32. Too Many Secrets, Too Many Lies, Sonya Sparks $15.00
33. Stick And Move, Shawn Black ($15.00) Coming 1/15/ 2008
34. Evil Side Of Money, Jeff Robertson $15.00
35. Cater To Her, W.S Burkett $15.00 Coming 3/30/ 2008
36. Blood of my Brother, Zoe & Ysuf Woods $15.00
37. Hoodfellas, Richard Jeanty $15.00 11/30/2008
38. The Bedroom Bandit, Richard Jeanty $15.00 March 2009
39. Stick N Move II, Shawn Black $15.00 April 2009
40. Miami Noire, W.S. Burkett $15.00 June 2009
41. Insanely In Love, Cereka Cook $15.00 May 2009
42. Blood of My Brother III, Zoe & Yusuf Woods August 2009

Name_____
Address_____
City_____State_____Zip Code_____

Please send the novels that I have circled above.

Shipping and Handling: Free
Total Number of Books_____
Total Amount Due_____

Buy 3 books and get 1 free. This offer is subject to change without notice.

Send institution check or money order (no cash or CODs) to:
RJ Publications
PO Box 300771
Jamaica, NY 11434

For more information please call 718-471-2926, or visit www.rjpublications.com

Please allow 2-3 weeks for delivery.

PUBLICATIONS
BRINGING EXCITEMENT, FUN AND JOY TO READING

Use this coupon to order by mail

43. Neglected Souls, Richard Jeanty $14.95
44. Neglected No More, Richard Jeanty $14.95
45. Sexual Exploits of Nympho, Richard Jeanty $14.95
46. Meeting Ms. Right's Whip Appeal, Richard Jeanty $14.95
47. Me and Mrs. Jones, K.M Thompson ($14.95) Available
48. Chasin' Satisfaction, W.S Burkett ($14.95) Available
49. Extreme Circumstances, Cereka Cook ($14.95) Available
50. The Most Dangerous Gang In America, R. Jeanty $15.00
51. Sexual Exploits of a Nympho II, Richard Jeanty $15.00
52. Sexual Jeopardy, Richard Jeanty $14.95 Coming: 2/15/ 2008
53. Too Many Secrets, Too Many Lies, Sonya Sparks $15.00
54. Stick And Move, Shawn Black ($15.00) Coming 1/15/ 2008
55. Evil Side Of Money, Jeff Robertson $15.00
56. Cater To Her, W.S Burkett $15.00 Coming 3/30/ 2008
57. Blood of my Brother, Zoe & Ysuf Woods $15.00
58. Hoodfellas, Richard Jeanty $15.00 11/30/2008
59. The Bedroom Bandit, Richard Jeanty $15.00 March 2009
60. Stick N Move II, Shawn Black $15.00 April 2009
61. Miami Noire, W.S. Burkett $15.00 June 2009
62. Insanely In Love, Cereka Cook $15.00 May 2009
63. Blood of My Brother III, Zoe & Yusuf Woods August 2009

Name_____
Address_____
City_____State_____Zip Code_____

Please send the novels that I have circled above.

Shipping and Handling: Free
Total Number of Books_____
Total Amount Due_____

Buy 3 books and get 1 free. This offer is subject to change without notice.

Send institution check or money order (no cash or CODs) to:
RJ Publications
PO Box 300771
Jamaica, NY 11434

For more information please call 718-471-2926, or visit www.rjpublications.com

Please allow 2-3 weeks for delivery.

PUBLICATIONS
BRINGING EXCITEMENT, FUN AND JOY TO READING

Use this coupon to order by mail

64. Neglected Souls, Richard Jeanty $14.95
65. Neglected No More, Richard Jeanty $14.95
66. Sexual Exploits of Nympho, Richard Jeanty $14.95
67. Meeting Ms. Right's Whip Appeal, Richard Jeanty $14.95
68. Me and Mrs. Jones, K.M Thompson ($14.95) Available
69. Chasin' Satisfaction, W.S Burkett ($14.95) Available
70. Extreme Circumstances, Cereka Cook ($14.95) Available
71. The Most Dangerous Gang In America, R. Jeanty $15.00
72. Sexual Exploits of a Nympho II, Richard Jeanty $15.00
73. Sexual Jeopardy, Richard Jeanty $14.95 Coming: 2/15/ 2008
74. Too Many Secrets, Too Many Lies, Sonya Sparks $15.00
75. Stick And Move, Shawn Black ($15.00) Coming 1/15/ 2008
76. Evil Side Of Money, Jeff Robertson $15.00
77. Cater To Her, W.S Burkett $15.00 Coming 3/30/ 2008
78. Blood of my Brother, Zoe & Ysuf Woods $15.00
79. Hoodfellas, Richard Jeanty $15.00 11/30/2008
80. The Bedroom Bandit, Richard Jeanty $15.00 March 2009
81. Stick N Move II, Shawn Black $15.00 April 2009
82. Miami Noire, W.S. Burkett $15.00 June 2009
83. Insanely In Love, Cereka Cook $15.00 May 2009
84. Blood of My Brother III, Zoe & Yusuf Woods August 2009

Name_____

Address_____

City_____State_____Zip Code_____

Please send the novels that I have circled above.

Shipping and Handling: Free
Total Number of Books_____
Total Amount Due_____

Buy 3 books and get 1 free. This offer is subject to change without notice.

Send institution check or money order (no cash or CODs) to:
RJ Publications
PO Box 300771
Jamaica, NY 11434

For more information please call 718-471-2926, or visit www.rjpublications.com

Please allow 2-3 weeks for delivery.

PUBLICATIONS
BRINGING EXCITEMENT, FUN AND JOY TO READING

Use this coupon to order by mail

85. Neglected Souls, Richard Jeanty $14.95
86. Neglected No More, Richard Jeanty $14.95
87. Sexual Exploits of Nympho, Richard Jeanty $14.95
88. Meeting Ms. Right's Whip Appeal, Richard Jeanty $14.95
89. Me and Mrs. Jones, K.M Thompson ($14.95) Available
90. Chasin' Satisfaction, W.S Burkett ($14.95) Available
91. Extreme Circumstances, Cereka Cook ($14.95) Available
92. The Most Dangerous Gang In America, R. Jeanty $15.00
93. Sexual Exploits of a Nympho II, Richard Jeanty $15.00
94. Sexual Jeopardy, Richard Jeanty $14.95 Coming: 2/15/ 2008
95. Too Many Secrets, Too Many Lies, Sonya Sparks $15.00
96. Stick And Move, Shawn Black ($15.00) Coming 1/15/ 2008
97. Evil Side Of Money, Jeff Robertson $15.00
98. Cater To Her, W.S Burkett $15.00 Coming 3/30/ 2008
99. Blood of my Brother, Zoe & Ysuf Woods $15.00
100. Hoodfellas, Richard Jeanty $15.00 11/30/2008
101. The Bedroom Bandit, Richard Jeanty $15.00 March 2009
102. Stick N Move II, Shawn Black $15.00 April 2009
103. Miami Noire, W.S. Burkett $15.00 June 2009
104. Insanely In Love, Cereka Cook $15.00 May 2009
105. Blood of My Brother III, Zoe & Yusuf Woods August 2009

Name_____
Address_____
City_____State_____Zip Code_____

Please send the novels that I have circled above.

Shipping and Handling: Free
Total Number of Books_____
Total Amount Due_____

Buy 3 books and get 1 free. This offer is subject to change without notice.

Send institution check or money order (no cash or CODs) to:
RJ Publications
PO Box 300771
Jamaica, NY 11434

For more information please call 718-471-2926, or visit www.rjpublications.com

Please allow 2-3 weeks for delivery.

PUBLICATIONS
BRINGING EXCITEMENT, FUN AND JOY TO READING

Use this coupon to order by mail

106. Neglected Souls, Richard Jeanty $14.95
107. Neglected No More, Richard Jeanty $14.95
108. Sexual Exploits of Nympho, Richard Jeanty $14.95
109. Meeting Ms. Right's Whip Appeal, Richard Jeanty $14.95
110. Me and Mrs. Jones, K.M Thompson ($14.95) Available
111. Chasin' Satisfaction, W.S Burkett ($14.95) Available
112. Extreme Circumstances, Cereka Cook ($14.95) Available
113. The Most Dangerous Gang In America, R. Jeanty $15.00
114. Sexual Exploits of a Nympho II, Richard Jeanty $15.00
115. Sexual Jeopardy, Richard Jeanty $14.95 Coming: 2/15/ 2008
116. Too Many Secrets, Too Many Lies, Sonya Sparks $15.00
117. Stick And Move, Shawn Black ($15.00) Coming 1/15/ 2008
118. Evil Side Of Money, Jeff Robertson $15.00
119. Cater To Her, W.S Burkett $15.00 Coming 3/30/ 2008
120. Blood of my Brother, Zoe & Ysuf Woods $15.00
121. Hoodfellas, Richard Jeanty $15.00 11/30/2008
122. The Bedroom Bandit, Richard Jeanty $15.00 March 2009
123. Stick N Move II, Shawn Black $15.00 April 2009
124. Miami Noire, W.S. Burkett $15.00 June 2009
125. Insanely In Love, Cereka Cook $15.00 May 2009
126. Blood of My Brother III, Zoe & Yusuf Woods August 2009

Name_____
Address_____
City_____State_____Zip Code_____

Please send the novels that I have circled above.

Shipping and Handling: Free
Total Number of Books_____
Total Amount Due_____

Buy 3 books and get 1 free. This offer is subject to change without notice.

Send institution check or money order (no cash or CODs) to:
RJ Publications
PO Box 300771
Jamaica, NY 11434

For more information please call 718-471-2926, or visit www.rjpublications.com

Please allow 2-3 weeks for delivery.